Bannock's Brand

LEO P. KELLEY

Bannock's Brand

A DOUBLE D WESTERN
DOUBLEDAY
New York London Toronto Sydney Auckland

A Double D Western
PUBLISHED BY DOUBLEDAY
a division of Bantam Doubleday Dell Publishing Group, Inc.
666 Fifth Avenue, New York, New York 10103

A Double D Western, Doubleday,
and the portrayal of the letters DD
are trademarks of Doubleday, a division of
Bantam Doubleday Dell Publishing Group, Inc.

Library of Congress Cataloging-in-Publication Data

Kelley, Leo P.
Bannock's brand/by Leo P. Kelley.—1st ed.
p.   cm. — (A Double D western)
I. Title.
PS3561.E388B3   1991
813'.54—dc20   90-47562
CIP

ISBN 0-385-41496-x
Copyright © 1991 by Leo P. Kelley
All Rights Reserved
Printed in the United States of America
April 1991
First Edition

10 9 8 7 6 5 4 3 2 1

Bannock's Brand

ONE

THE SUN BLAZED DOWN upon the lean body of the lone man as he rode north toward the Texas border and Indian Territory, which lay beyond it. His rawboned face was in shadow as a result of his having pulled the brim of his flat-topped black Stetson down low on his forehead. Nevertheless sweat gave it a sheen and made dark damp marks on the back of his blue cotton shirt.

The hot sun had its silent effect upon the man's roan too. The horse moved at a slow pace, its gait almost somnolent. Sweat glistened on its hide. The saliva that had been slipping from between its lips before the sun rose no longer appeared, testifying to the dryness of the animal's mouth.

The rider barely moved in his bullet-scarred saddle as the horse under him plodded on. Around him stretched the prairie dotted here and there with stands of post oaks and elms. Under his horse's hooves grew coarse bunch grass mixed with some bush muhly and tobosa.

He sat his saddle as if he were riding through the coolest spring day, as if the relentless sun assaulting him and his mount made no difference to him. His tall body, as slender as it was strong, was relaxed but in no way indolent. Although there was no tension in it there was a clear readiness to move and move fast if action became necessary. His blue eyes were alert but not uneasy. They took in the sun-blinded world around him with a kind of wary record-keeping. Nothing escaped their notice. His straight hair was the color of pitch and it had not known a barber's touch in some time. Nor had his stubbled cheeks and chin.

His eyes caught movement in a patch of tobosa directly ahead of him. At the same instant, he felt his roan's body begin to tremble. He tightened his grip on the reins to keep the horse from bolting as the tobosa moved again and a sidewinder came into view as it slithered through the dry growth.

The roan tossed its head, fighting the bit. The rider drew rein and brought the horse to a halt. It high-stepped, its great eyes rolling as they filled with fear.

"Easy," the rider said softly. He reached out and stroked his mount's neck. "Nice and easy, that's the way to take it. That snake's not going to bite you," he practically purred, just loud enough to be heard by the horse. His hand slid smoothly along the animal's tense and sweaty neck. Within moments, he felt his mount begin to relax as the sidewinder moved farther away. The flesh of the roan's neck no longer rippled nervously under his touch. The animal seemed to welcome the warmth of the rider's gentling hand. It nickered.

"I know. We're having about as much fun out here in this hot-as-the-hinges-of-hell sun as a baby with a bellyache. Tell you what. We'll head east a bit—over to where those post oaks'll give us some shelter for a spell. How's that strike you, old fellow?" He used knee pressure to turn his roan and then walked the horse toward the trees.

The rider's name was Ben Bannock. His jeans were worn and faded and his low-heeled black army boots were thick with trail dust. The blue bandanna he wore around the corded column of his neck was soaked with sweat.

Around his lean hips he wore a black leather cartridge belt, every loop of which was filled. From the belt hung an equally black leather holster which housed his .44-caliber single-action six-shot Smith and Wesson army revolver, from which he had cut away the trigger guard to make for a faster draw. He had

oiled the inside of his holster for the same reason. The stock of a
Henry rifle protruded from a saddle scabbard.

When he reached the trees, he rode in among them and
almost immediately felt relief in the relatively cool shadows
filling the small forest. His horse nickered again as if to com-
ment on the respite the trees offered from the burning sun.

When Bannock spotted a stand of burdock in the distance, he
moved his horse toward it. He drew rein beside the plants,
which were thriving in an open area filled with sunlight, their
rhubarb-like leaves growing on long tough stems. The tallest of
the plants was, Bannock estimated, a good seven feet tall while
the younger ones stood less than three feet.

He dismounted and pulled up several of the younger plants.
He tore off their stalks, rubbed their bulbs on his jeans to rid
them of as much dirt as possible and began to eat them raw.
Slowly the hunger that had been gnawing at him began to sub-
side. He finished his meal by eating some of the pith of the
burdock plants' stalks, reminding him of the long ago years
when he had been a boy and the pith of burdock plants had been
used by his mother as a bribe to stir her sometimes indolent son
into doing his assigned chores. The pith was as much of a treat
to the boy Bannock had been then as was the colorful penny
candy bought at the mercantile in town.

He took his canteen down from his saddle horn, opened it
and drank. What water remained in the canteen, he poured into
his hat and gave to his roan to drink. Deciding that his horse
needed a rest, he let the animal browse. While waiting for it to
satisfy its own hunger, he hunkered down with his back braced
against the trunk of a post oak and his forearms propped on his
knees, letting his strong-fingered hands hang down in front of
him.

Bannock listened to what most men would call the silence
surrounding him. But Bannock, where most men would hear
only silence, heard the light breeze easing through the branches
of the trees above his head, its soft passage an almost inaudible
whisper. He heard the sound of an invisible beetle scurrying

through some fallen leaves. He heard the *tap-tap, tap-tap* of a branch lightly brushing against another one some thirty yards away.

He closed his eyes, his hunger satisfied, his mind at ease and his heart almost content. His mind roamed back to the homeplace where he had grown up. To his ma and pa. To his pa, who had taught him all the skills a man needed to know to survive in what was, by anyone's reckoning, an untamed world. And to his ma, who had taught him that there were, nevertheless, touches of gentility in that wild world as well. A smile crept across his face in the wake of his memories.

Some time later, the sounds his roan was making as it browsed the underbrush beneath the trees broke into Bannock's reverie. He opened his eyes and stood up. He went to his horse, tightened his cinch and rode on through the forest, still heading north toward the border.

Later, as he emerged from the trees, he heard the shriek of a train whistle as it tore across the plains, thick black smoke rising from its funnel. He watched the train head south along the tracks of the Missouri Kansas and Texas railroad, called the Katy by most people. He rode parallel to the tracks leaving the train far behind him, its whistle gradually fading into silence.

The sun, red as blood, was almost down by the time he arrived in the border settlement of Pinetown in Cherokee Nation. The town, he noted, was in a kind of transitional state. Not exactly quiet but far from rowdy. The townspeople were home, most of them, gathered around their supper tables. The men and women of the night, the merrymakers as well as those who knew that making merry was a thing of the past for them and sought only to drown their bitter knowledge, would not appear until darkness filled the streets and stars the sky.

He drew rein beside a feed lot and holding pen on the western edge of town and sat his saddle, hands wrapped around his saddle horn, and stared at the cattle in the pen. Good stock, his experienced eye told him. All of them were longhorns—long-legged and sturdy. Most of them were somewhat lean, which suggested that they'd been on the trail awhile. There were some blooded Durhams among them and their influence on the breeding program of whoever owned them was evident in the fact that many of the younger longhorns were meatier and more low slung in build than was the case with the native stock.

He spurred his horse and rode on down the street, the clattering of the cattle's horns a brittle music in his ears. He turned left and soon found himself in the town's main street. He brought his horse to a halt in front of the Paradise Saloon. He got out of the saddle, looped the roan's reins around the hitch rail in front of the saloon and went inside.

The place was almost empty. A man, his head cradled on arms which were folded across a table near the bar, snored. There were no women in sight. Two men played poker in the last of the sun's dying light that filtered through a begrimed window next to the door.

Bannock made his way to the oak bar, hooked a boot heel on the brass rail and ordered whiskey.

The bar dog poured a drink. "Two bits," the sleeve-gartered and mustachioed man said in a voice dulled by boredom.

Bannock dug some coins from the pocket of his worn jeans and placed them in a pile on the bar. The bar dog took from it what was due him and placed it in his till.

Bannock downed his drink and ordered another. He stood there, most of his weight resting on his one foot that was on the floor, and stared into his glass. He could still see the cattle in the holding pen on the edge of town and he imagined he could still hear the clattering of their horns.

He took a taste of his second drink as the poker players left and were replaced by two elderly men who drank gin as they played dominoes. The clattering of the dominoes drowned out the remembered sound of the steers' clattering horns, which had been loud in Bannock's mind.

The whiskey tasted bitter. It burned its way down his throat and sat heavily in his gut. But its fire burned away the aches and stiffness that the long trails he had been riding had left him as their legacy. The whiskey even made him feel almost at peace with himself.

Hours later, when the pile of coins in front of him was almost gone and the saloon was crowded to overflowing, a man shouldered his way between Bannock and a woman wearing a faded yellow silk dress.

"I'm buying," the man said, his speech slightly slurred. "What'samatter, you deef?" he asked sullenly when Bannock made no response.

Bannock gave him a sidelong look. The man was young—twenty or thereabouts—with a short blocky build. He wore the clothes of a trail hand and his face was sunburned and pitted with scars that spoke of a bout with the pox. His eyes were a watery blue, their whites red-veined. There was anger in them and in his voice. He weighed, Bannock estimated, one-seventy, one-eighty. About the same as me, he thought. But he's short and blocky.

The man repeated his question, the anger Bannock had seen lurking in his eyes flaring into full view.

"No, I'm not deaf," Bannock said.

"Bar dog!" the man next to him shouted and beckoned. When the bar dog arrived in front of his increasingly belligerent customer, the man pointed to Bannock's empty glass and said, "Give him one on me."

As the bar dog was about to refill the glass, Bannock placed a hand over it and shook his head. "I've reached my limit."

"You sure enough ain't the sociable type now, are you?" the young man muttered, gazing at Bannock through narrowed eyes. "What's the matter with you? Maybe you don't like my looks, is that it?"

"I've got nothing against you. I just would appreciate it if you would mind your business and let me mind mine."

"D'you hear him?" the young man remarked in an overloud voice. "This surly fella thinks he's too damn good for the likes of Curly Lassiter."

"Leave it be, Curly," said an older man who suddenly appeared at Lassiter's side. He gripped the younger man's arm and said, "Let's go somewheres else, Curly, what'a'ya say?"

"I'm content right here where I am," Lassiter responded and shook off the older man's hand. "Or I would be if this barn-shouldered bastard here knew how to treat a friendly offer to buy him a drink."

As Bannock and the man behind Lassiter exchanged glances, Bannock said, "Take your friend out of here, mister, before there's trouble."

"Come on, Curly. Let's go."

"I'm not going nowhere! Not until I buy this surly sonofa-bitch a drink."

"Curly, come on. This fella, he don't want no drink. Besides he's packing a gun and you ain't."

"You think he's fixing to shoot me, do you?" Lassiter asked, assuming an exaggerated expression of abject fear and holding up his hands as if to ward off a round from Bannock's six-gun. When he spoke again, his tone was icy. "Put away that gun, mister, and I'll teach you how to act sociable next time some-body wants to buy you a drink."

"I don't want to fight you," Bannock said flatly.

"You hear that?" Lassiter whooped to his uneasy companion. "He's yellow-bellied, just like I thought all along—right from his word one."

Bannock, fighting down the fury that the younger man's taunts had spawned in him, kept his face expressionless as he reached out to pick up the few coins of his which remained on the bar.

Before he could do so, the younger man's hand snaked out and sent the coins scattering to the floor behind the bar.

Bannock stared at the spot where they had been. His body was stiff, his muscles taut. He straightened, removed his foot from the brass rail, unbuckled his gunbelt and carefully placed it on the bar where the coins had been. Then, turning to the younger man who was grinning lopsidedly and watching him carefully, he said, "You've been pining for a fight, Lassiter. Well, boy, I'm

about to give you one that I reckon you'll remember for the rest
of your life."

"Don't you call me 'boy'!" Lassiter screamed, his face redden-
ing. "I'm as much a man as you are and I'm fixing to prove that
right this very minute." Lassiter threw a clumsy right cross
which only grazed Bannock's left shoulder.

Before Lassiter could strike again or even withdraw his fist,
Bannock let go with a roundhouse right that slammed into the
younger man's face and sent his head snapping to the side.

The blow seemed to stun Lassiter momentarily. He raised a
hand and gingerly touched the spot where Bannock's fist had
landed and stared at his opponent as if seeing him for the first
time. Then he snarled and lunged at Bannock, both fists flailing
wildly.

Lassiter's left uppercut struck Bannock's chin but Bannock,
seeing it coming, had taken a step backward so that the blow lost
some of its force. Bannock took another step backward. Then,
raising his fists and circling Lassiter, he led the younger man out
into the middle of the barroom and away from the spectators
who were eagerly watching the fight and urging both men on.
Bannock waited for the right moment, still circling, and it came
when Lassiter, enraged at what he apparently perceived as Bannock's stalling tactics, bellowed, "Stand your ground and fight
like a man, you bastard!"

As Lassiter came at him, Bannock delivered a savage series of
blows, one after the other, that buried themselves in Lassiter's
gut. They knocked the air out of the man's lungs and sent him
staggering backward to fall over and shatter a table.

Bannock was on him in an instant, dragging him to his feet
with his left hand and smashing his right fist into his face time
and time again. Lassiter's head snapped right, then, left, then
right again. Blood burst from his split lower lip. His broken
nose spurted blood, joining the flow from his lip which covered
his stubbled chin.

Undeterred by his injuries, Lassiter went for Bannock again.
This time his thumbs tried to gouge out Bannock's eyes. Ban-

nock defended himself by raising both of his arms between those of Lassiter and then snapping them outward, sending Lassiter's arms flying to the sides.

Lassiter kicked him in the left shin. As pain racketed through Bannock's leg, Lassiter danced around behind him and, with the fingers of both of his hands locked together to form one hard fist, he brought that fist down on the base of Bannock's skull, knocking Bannock to his knees. Lassiter crouched and proceeded to deliver a savage blow to Bannock's kidneys. Bannock grunted, turned, started to rise—and found Lassiter's booted right foot flying through the air toward his face. He reached up and caught it in both of his hands. He twisted it as hard and as fast as he could and Lassiter shouted an obscenity as he went down hard on the barroom floor.

Bannock sprang to his feet and stood waiting for Lassiter to rise. At first, the man seemed unable or unwilling to get to his feet. He lay there, propped up on one elbow, staring balefully up at Bannock as he wiped the sweat from his eyes and then some of the blood from his chin.

"I'm willing to call it quits if you are," Bannock told him as he sucked air into his burning lungs.

Lassiter's response was an animalistic snarl. He scuttled across the floor and when he came up he had a wooden chair in his hands, which he threw at Bannock.

But Bannock ducked and the chair sailed over his head to smash into the rows of bottles behind the bar, breaking most of them.

"Stop them!" the irate bar dog bellowed, shaking both fists at the two men who were once again warily circling one another. "Somebody get the marshal before they wreck this place altogether!"

Lassiter threw a wild punch. Bannock chopped down upon it with his right fist and then struck Lassiter with his left. Lassiter grunted. Lowering his head, he ran at Bannock, butting him like an enraged billy goat. Bannock seized him by the shoulders and sent him spinning across the room, his arms waving wildly as if his hands were seeking something substantial to grasp in an attempt to halt his headlong flight. Lassiter slammed into the far wall and his hands landed flat upon it, the one he had used to wipe the blood from his chin leaving a bloody smear. Lassiter sank to his knees with his forehead leaning against the wall.

Bannock stood there, his chest heaving and his fists aching. He blinked the sweat out of his eyes which was blurring his vision. Damn fool kid, he thought. Has to prove himself a man in front of the watching world. If he were a man, he wouldn't have had to start this damn foolishness in the first place. He waited, watching Lassiter claw his way up the wall and then turn to face him again, hate in his eyes. But there was something else in them also, Bannock saw, and he knew the name of that something else: respect for his opponent. Bannock almost smiled. Instead he warily watched Lassiter as the man moved toward him, his gait somewhat unsteady, his fists trembling slightly. Here we go again, he thought, and wished he were a million miles away.

Lassiter swung. And swung again.

Neither blow landed because Bannock had eased backward from the waist. All he felt was the slight breeze the blows had sent swirling past his face. Lassiter shook his head trying to clear it. Drops of blood spattered on Bannock's face as he did so. Bannock stood his ground. He threw no punches. He hoped that Lassiter was about to give up.

But Lassiter didn't give up. Instead he lowered his head and lunged at Bannock, both hands desperately grasping. One clawed Bannock's right cheek, drawing three thin lines of blood, and the other seized Bannock's shirt and ripped it, popping buttons and revealing Bannock's broad chest and the brand that was burned on it: ⲂⲂ. A double B.

Lassiter proceeded to pummel Bannock, his ribs, his gut, his groin. Bannock knocked the man's fists away from his body and then he grabbed Lassiter by the scruff of the neck and the seat of the pants, lifted him high above his head and threw him against the bar.

The spectators who had been cheering and egging the battling men on, suddenly fell silent. All of their eyes were on the man who lay draped across the brass rail, his clothes stained by the contents of a brass spittoon he had overturned when he landed.

Bannock, as a wave of weakness suddenly washed over him, reached out and got a grip on the banister of the stairs that led to the second floor. The room began to whirl around him. He felt his knees go weak and he wondered if he was going to go down.

Lassiter stood up. He held onto the bar to steady himself. He raised his head and stared at Bannock.

Bannock willed himself to remain standing. He demanded that his heart hold steady and that his will not weaken. He watched, blinking, through a haze of eye-searing cigar smoke as Lassiter weaved his way toward him. He didn't move as Lassiter swung at him. He took the weak blow that he knew was the younger man's last effort and then watched as Lassiter swayed, opened his mouth to say something and then fell in an unconscious heap in front of Bannock's boots.

"You beat him!" one of the watching men exclaimed, and another shouted, "You sure were hell on the hoof, mister, whoever you are! You put Curly in his place all right."

Bannock felt neither pleasure nor satisfaction at the outcome of the fight. He hadn't wanted to fight in the first place but he had been forced to do so. Now it was over and nobody had won anything. There was a bloody taste in his mouth and a heaviness in his heart. He limped toward the bar, favoring the leg that Lassiter had kicked early on in the battle. He was in the act of picking up his gunbelt when a harsh voice that came from behind him said, "Hold it!"

He froze. One of Lassiter's friends ready to take over for the downed warrior? He almost sighed.

"Turn around!" from the same male voice which had just spoken.

Bannock slowly turned around to find himself facing a man

with a marshal's badge pinned to his leather vest and a Colt
Peacemaker in his hand.

"It's time you were on your way, mister," the marshal barked.
"This here's a peaceable town. We don't have any use for the
likes of brawlers like you."

"He jumped Curly, Marshal," declared the man who had
earlier tried to persuade Lassiter to leave the saloon. "Had
himself no reason in the world to act like he did, Marshal. Why,
he near beat the poor boy to death as you can plainly see for
your own self. Curly's daddy is gonna pitch a fit when he finds
out what this jasper has went and done to his pride and joy."

"You hear that, mister?" the marshal said to Bannock. "The
Lassiters are a respected family in these parts. Old Jess Lassiter
—he's Curly's daddy—he might take a notion to come gunning
for a man who did that to his son." The marshal pointed to the
bloody face of the still unconscious Lassiter. "My advice to you
is get out of town and get out right now if you know what's good
for you."

Bannock nodded and this time he did sigh, a sound that was
part sorrow and part resignation. He watched the lawman's eyes
drop to the Double B burned into the flesh of his chest. He saw
the marshal wince, imagining what it must have been like to
have a red-hot branding iron lifted from a fire, brought toward
you, pressed down hard on your bare chest, searing it, the
pungent stench of your own roasted flesh filling your nostrils . . .

"I'm going," Bannock said. He picked up his gunbelt and
limped toward the batwings.

"Don't come back to Pinetown any time soon, mister!" the
marshal called out to him as Bannock shouldered his way
through the batwings and went outside into the town's by now
rowdy night.

Wagons and carriages careened down Pinetown's wide main
street. Men stood on street corners talking, laughing, clapping
one another on the back. Women were scarce but those who
leaned out of second-story windows or strolled up and down the

street had eyes that invited and bodies clad in skimpy, short-skirted clothes.

Bannock crossed the street and entered a store that was brightly lit and which had a sign above its door which read: Dry Goods.

"Yes, sir?" chirped a bespectacled clerk from behind the counter as he pushed his sleeve garters higher up on his arms. "What can I do for you, sir?"

Before Bannock could answer the question, the clerk's eyes widened and his face paled. He stared at the scarred flesh of Bannock's chest visible through the tatters that were all that remained of his shirt.

"I'm in need of a shirt."

The clerk looked up. "A shirt. Oh yes, a shirt." He turned and rummaged about on a shelf until he found a box tied with store string. He took it down and placed it on the counter. Removing the string and lifting the lid, he displayed the contents of the box to Bannock.

"Mind if I try this one?" Bannock asked, taking a blue and red checkered shirt out of the box. "Want to make sure it fits."

"Go right ahead, sir."

Bannock stripped off the remains of the shirt he was wearing and slipped into the new one he had taken from the box. He was buttoning it when a woman rounded a counter and stopped in her tracks at the sight of him—at the sight of the brand he bore on his chest.

He ignored her audible gasp and told the clerk, "It's a bit tight across the shoulders but it beats the other one I came in here wearing by a country mile. How much?"

"Sixty-five cents, sir."

Bannock handed over the money.

"Will that be all, sir? We have a sale on trousers this week."

"I'm not in need of any. So far these Frisco jeans have kept me in and the wind out."

Once outside again, Bannock recrossed the street and entered the general store. "I'll have two pounds of salt pork, some bread, a couple of cans of tomatoes and one of peaches."

The clerk behind the counter darted from shelf to shelf and soon had Bannock's order piled up next to the cash box. He took a pencil from behind his ear and a piece of butcher paper from a roll and began to add up the charges for the items ordered.

"That comes to a grand total of two dollars and thirty-two cents."

Bannock reached out and picked up the paper the clerk had been writing on. He quickly scanned it, calculating. "You made a mistake. The grand total's two dollars and *twenty*-two cents."

The clerk took the paper from him, examined it and then grinned sheepishly. "You're 100 percent right. Two dollars and *twenty*-two cents it is."

Bannock paid what he owed and the clerk packed his purchases in a brown paper sack.

Carrying the sack, Bannock left the store, crossed the street to where his horse stood and packed the items he had bought in his saddlebags. Then, swinging into the saddle, he walked his roan down the main street and out into the night now lurking just beyond the reach of Pinetown's lamplight.

The moon rose as he rode on. It's as fat and full as a cat that's just finished lapping up a whole bowlful of cream, he thought, looking up at it. Maybe the moon's the reason for the ruckus I got dragged into back there in town. A full moon does seem to have a way of setting wolves to baying and young upstarts like that Curly Lassiter to brawling.

He scanned the moonlit landscape as he rode, searching for a good place to make camp for the night. Someplace where there was wood and water. He had found none by the time he came to the Red River. So he rode along the river's bank for a short distance until he came to a spot that looked like an easy ford. He moved his horse into the water, noting as he did so that it did not appear to be its normal reddish-brown color as a result of the moon's light upon it. The moon's made magic, he thought. It's turned the Red into a slick silver ribbon.

As he continued fording the river, he saw pieces of cloth and driftwood caught in the uppermost branches of some cottonwoods growing along the bank. They bore mute but eloquent testimony to the power of the Red when it reached flood stage. And it often did, he knew. Unseen storms occurring in the western mountains could turn it into a raging flood in a matter of hours. Bannock had seen the river rise from a wadable six inches to twenty-five feet in a day's time.

He remembered the time, during a cattle drive heading north to the railhead at Abilene, when some of his cows had become caught in the Red's treacherous quicksand. He and his men had succeeded in trussing the mired animals and hauling them safely out of the river. All but the one that had lost a leg when the rope the drovers had turned around the hub of the chuck wagon's wheel that served as a capstan had slipped. Bannock had been the one who put a bullet in the cow's brain. He remembered . . .

He set his thought aside. That was the past. Better to bury it.

He rode out of the river and up onto dry land. He had not gone far into Indian Territory when he heard it.

The sound of someone splashing through the river behind him.

Curly Lassiter come to get even with him for the beating he'd taken?

Bannock recalled a remark the marshal had made following the fight. Something about Jess Lassiter, Curly's daddy, coming after the man who had mistreated his son.

Bannock drew rein and listened. Was it only one rider coming up behind him? He dismounted and put his ear to the ground. He heard a horse come out of the water onto dry land. One rider, no doubt about that. He got up and led his horse around a bend. Leaving it ground-hitched, he climbed up the sloping face of a limestone hill and dropped down behind an outcropping

near its top. Taking off his hat and drawing his revolver, he
waited, watching the land below him.

Within minutes, a lone rider came into sight. He wore a felt
hat that shadowed his face, hiding his features. It could be
Lassiter, Bannock decided. Or his daddy. He circled around and
came down from the limestone hill. He loped along the trail left
by his and the other rider's horses until he was within sight of
the rider who was now directly ahead of him.

"Hold it!" he called out. "Hold it right there and raise your
hands high!"

The rider halted his horse. Slowly, his hands rose. "You fixing
to backshoot me, mister?"

The voice wasn't Curly Lassiter's. But it could be the voice of
Jess Lassiter, Curly's daddy, which Bannock had never heard.
He moved forward cautiously. When he reached the rider he
moved around in front of him and thumbed back the hammer of
his gun.

TWO

"DON'T SHOOT!" the stranger yelped.

Bannock kept his thumb on the hammer of his .44 as he studied the rider.

He was close enough to him now to see by the light of the moon that he was confronting not a man but a mere boy. Maybe the kid was thirteen. Fourteen tops. He had dusky skin but he didn't look like an Indian. Not dark enough. Too straight a nose. His lips were full and the skin of his face hadn't yet known the touch of a razor. He had eyes—frightened eyes at the moment— that were as blue as Bannock's own. Black hair, straight and sleek. He was a well-built youngster, made mostly of sinew and muscle without an extra ounce of fat on him anywhere.

"Are you going to shoot me?"

Instead of answering the boy's question, Bannock asked one of his own. "What are you doing here?"

"Nothing."

"Where'd you come from?"

"Back there." The boy, whose voice had the faintest trace of an accent of some kind, jerked a thumb over his shoulder. "I just left Pinetown and was heading north."

"On my backtrail. In the dark."

"I've got a right to ride where and when I please and you're not going to tell me otherwise."

Bannock heard the unmistakable note of defiance that had sharpened the boy's voice. It amused him. Here this kid was facing a man with a loaded gun who might turn out to be some kind of desperado and he was telling that man in no uncertain terms that he had a right to be where he was and wasn't about to be run off. Apparently the kid had more guts than you could hang on a fence.

"Where you headed?"

"Yonder."

"That far, huh?" Bannock managed not to smile.

"Well, are you?"

"Am I what?"

"Going to drill me?"

Bannock had almost forgotten the six-gun in his hand. He holstered it. "Not tonight, I'm not."

"Then I'll put my hands down if that won't spook you into doing something silly like blowing my brains out."

As the boy lowered his hands, Bannock went to his horse and brought it back. "It so happens," he told the boy, "that I'm also heading yonder. You're welcome to ride along with me if you've a mind to."

"I don't know," the boy said hesitantly. "You're a touchy type, it appears to me. You just might take another notion to throw down on me like you just did."

"If you mind your manners and make no false moves, there won't be any further danger of that. You see, I'm a man who doesn't take too kindly to fellas who pop up out of nowhere in the middle of the night."

"It's not even ten o'clock yet. That's hardly the middle of the night."

Bannock decided he would have to speak more carefully. This kid was turning out to be a stickler for accuracy. He obviously had no poetry in his soul. It was no doubt stuffed full of nothing but cold dry facts.

Bannock stepped into the saddle and moved out. He looked over his shoulder and saw the kid sitting his saddle and watching him. Well, he thought, the boy's got no gun. So I won't get backshot. Unless he's packing a hideout gun. He put heels to his horse and was soon beyond the range of a derringer.

"You coming or are you fixing to stay there and sulk all night?" he called back over his shoulder.

The boy moved his horse out and was soon riding beside Bannock.

"I've been looking for a place to make camp for the night," Bannock remarked idly. "Haven't found one yet."

"There's a crick up ahead."

Bannock glanced at his companion. "You know this neck of the woods, do you?"

"I've been in and about it some."

"You live around here?"

"Nope. Just passing through."

"You've run off from your homeplace." A statement, not a question.

"You could say that."

"You like riding around out in the middle of nowhere in the dark of night without a nice feather bed to settle down into and a hot meal waiting for you come morning, is that it?"

"I've been adventuring."

"Oh, ho, that explains it."

"Explains what?"

"That you have a purpose in life and aren't just another forlorn stray I've picked up."

"I've been to Arizona. New Mexico too."

"You've spent a night or two in jail as well."

The boy gave Bannock a sidelong glance.

"Stands to reason. If you thought I was a mind reader, you were dead wrong. A boy wandering hither and yonder is bound to run out of money from time to time—"

"I work to support myself. I hayed for a farmer in Texas and I swamped a saloon in Yuma—"

"But you ran out of spending money now and then, I figured,

and along comes the law and locks you up for vagrancy. Isn't that a fact now?''

"I'm not saying if it is or if it isn't.''

So I was right, Bannock thought. Well, I guess it takes one saddle tramp to recognize another one, never mind the difference in their ages.

They rode on then in silence until they came to the creek that the boy had mentioned. There they dismounted and, without a word, the boy went in search of wood, leaving Bannock to lead their horses to the water where he let them drink their fill, since neither would be back on the trail for the rest of the night.

Later, after the boy had returned with dry wood from a deadfall and had a fire going beneath some trees, Bannock hunkered down opposite from where the boy was sitting cross-legged on the ground.

"I've got some beef jerky in my saddlebag,'' the boy volunteered. "You're welcome to some if you're hungry.''

"Beef jerky would be fine right about now. I'd planned on eating a meal in the restaurant back in Pinetown but—well, let's say things didn't work out for me back there so I lit a shuck and here I am.''

The boy got up and when he returned he handed some thin strips of jerky to Bannock and then resumed his position close to the fire.

Bannock bit into the tough jerky and began to chew it, surreptiously watching the boy seated on the ground across from him. The boy who was headed "yonder.'' The boy who had been out "adventuring.''

"What's your name?'' he asked.

"Tony.''

"Well, Tony, you remind me of myself when I wasn't much older than you are now. I also left home and went adventuring, as you call it, same as you've done.'' Bannock paused a moment. "They say''—he grinned—"the wilder the colt, the better the horse.''

Thinking back to those days as he sat staring into the fire,

Bannock found himself remembering both the good and the bad times he had experienced on the long and twisted trail that had led him to where he now was. . . .

Bannock stood beside his ranch foreman, Wes Holbrook, and watched as the branding of his calves that had been gathered in the spring roundup continued.

Cowboys on horseback yelped and *ki-yied* as they chased calves. Cows bawled as they became separated from their offspring. A mean-spirited steer charged one of the riders, almost goring the man's mount.

"The increase was good this year," Wes commented. "So far, we've tallied sixty-one calves. The Bannock ranch is growing by leaps and bounds. If things keep up like this—if we keep growing like we have been—we'll be bigger than the King ranch in a year or two's time. We will, that is, if we don't run into any serious trouble."

Bannock glanced at Wes. "Trouble? You're expecting some?"

"Well, there has been talk of trouble. I thought you might have heard some of it."

The bawling of a cow near the campfire distracted Bannock. He watched as the cow lumbered through the milling herd that had been gathered in the spring roundup. He knew she was searching for her calf from which she had apparently become separated during the gathering.

The cow stopped bawling as she practically collided with the calf she had been seeking. She nuzzled it and it promptly went for her bag and began to suck.

"Mr. Bannock!" One of the cowboys involved in the branding of the calves called out and beckoned to Bannock, who, with Wes at his side, walked over to the man.

"What is it, Slim?" Bannock asked.

Slim pointed to the brand on the calf's hide. "Phil McIntyre's got to that calf of ours before we could this spring. That's his Circle Diamond brand the critter's wearing."

"I'll have a word with McIntyre," Bannock said. "I'll tell him his calves ought not to be sucking Double B brand cows."

Holbrook laughed. Slim smiled.

"Slap our brand on that calf," Bannock ordered. "There's no doubt it belongs to us since its mother bears the Double B brand."

"Phil McIntyre's been known to gather unbranded calves that don't belong to him, Mr. Bannock. Last fall, we had trouble with him when we rode onto his range to search for strays. He had brand-blotted nearly a dozen of our stock."

"Like I said, I'll have a word with him. I ought to be able to straighten him out. If not, I'll sic the law on him, though that move would be one I'd make only as a last resort. I didn't spend all these years building up my herd to have it stolen out from under me bit by little bit."

"Eight years," Holbrook said, shaking his head in wonder. "It took you only eight years and you wound up with one of the best and biggest ranches in this part of the state. I wish I had the knack of doing things as slick and smooth as you do, Mr. Bannock. If I did, I wouldn't still be cowboying. I'd be a cattle baron same as yourself." A sigh. "You wouldn't consider trading places with me, would you?"

"Both jobs have their headaches, Wes, I can assure you. And a word of advice—don't be so quick to trade places with another man till you know all there is to know about him. You might find you've made yourself a bad bargain."

A calf bawled its pain for all the world to hear as one of Bannock's men rammed a cherry-red iron onto its hide. The smell of burned flesh and singed hair filled the air. Then, after a moment during which tendrils of smoke rose from the branded calf's skin, the cowboy sitting on the calf's head to hold it still rose and the other cowboy who had heel-caught it with his rope freed the animal's legs and rode off in search of another un-branded calf.

"I take it, Wes," Bannock said, "that the trouble you mentioned before had to do with the bravos."

"Yes, sir, that's right. The bravos were raising hell again last week. They raided a good number of miles north of the border. Put another way, they came within thirty miles of the Nueces River—and us."

"They never should have disbanded the Texas Rangers," Bannock remarked. "If they hadn't, we wouldn't have this problem."

"I have to say I think you hit the nail square on the head. They might come this far north next time, and if they do, we'll be right in the path of those damned rustlers."

"It's surprising to me that the Mexican Government doesn't take a stand against Colonel Mantavo and his bravos. It's as surprising to me that our own politicians here in Texas and those back east in Washington don't force the Mexican Government to stop Mantavo and his men in their tracks."

"Mantavo's a war hero, Mr. Bannock, as you no doubt know. Maybe that's why. He helped make mincemeat out of Santos Benavides's Confederate cavalry during the war and wound up as Colonel Pedro Mantavo, Commander of the Line of the Bravo. Now he's got his men stealing Texas cattle right and left and driving them across the border to sell at two to four dollars a head and here we stand around and wring our hands and don't do a damn thing about it."

"I mean to do something. I intend to defend the Bannock ranch against any and all attempts to raid it."

"Maybe we'll be lucky. Maybe they'll stick close to the border and not bother us."

"Maybe they will." But Bannock doubted it. Once the Mexican rustlers had thinned the herds south of his own ranch, he was sure they would drift farther and farther north in search of more cattle to ship to places like Cuba, where they brought top prices.

Bannock coughed as the wind suddenly gusted, sending the smoke into his nostrils and down his throat. He and Wes were silent then, both of them lost in their own thoughts, as they watched the branding continue.

One of the Bannock hands brought in a calf he had head-roped. He drew rein near the fire. Even before his mount had come to a full stop, a second man ran from the fire and got a grip on the mounted man's rope. He walked down the taut line until he had a hand on the noose around the roped calf's neck. He flipped the rope off, reached over the calf's back, grabbed a fistful of loose skin on the animal's side and pulled. At the same time, he kneed the calf's foreleg that was nearest to him out from under the frightened animal. The calf went down, the wind knocked out of it. The man who had upset the calf promptly sat down on its head as another man joined him and pushed the downed calf's underside hind leg forward with a booted foot and simultaneously pulled the topside hind leg toward him, thus baring the calf's scrotum.

Two more men joined the first two. One had a branding iron in his hands and, as he pressed it into the flesh of the downed calf, causing the animal to bawl in agony, a knife appeared in the hand of the second man who knelt and with one deft movement of his blade turned the calf into a steer.

The scrotum was tossed into a bucket to join other scrotums and parts of ears that had been cut off during ear marking. The branding iron was withdrawn. The calf was released and went racing away, still bawling its anguish, smoke rising from its burned flesh.

"Nice job," Bannock commented. "The brand was just deep enough. Any deeper and it would have set the animal's hair on fire."

The work continued for another hour. At the end of that time, Slim rejoined Bannock and Wes and, consulting his tally book, announced, "Boss, we branded sixty-seven calves and eleven yearlings all told. As far as we can tell, we got 'em all. Though there may be a few strays still at large that the boys missed in the gathering."

"Fine work, Slim. I thank you and the other men for a job well done."

"Tomorrow we're going to treat a few cases of lump jaw we

found and dehorn some of the steers before they gouge holes in their friends and relatives with their overgrown crowning glories. But now, if it's all right with you, me and the boys thought we'd have us a little fun."

"I don't see any women around," Wes commented, ostentatiously rolling his eyes for Slim's benefit.

"I'm not talking about that kind of fun." Turning to Bannock, Slim continued, "This foreman of yours, boss, he's got only two things on his mind. His belly and his balls."

Bannock laughed good-naturedly. "What kind of fun did you have in mind?"

"Barney's come up with another one of his crackpot ideas," Slim replied. "This time he's proposed a cow-milking contest."

Bannock and Wes exchanged puzzled glances.

"A cow-milking contest?" an incredulous Wes asked.

Slim held up a bony finger. "Hold on, Wes. Don't go getting your exercise by jumping to conclusions. This idea of Barney's —it's no ordinary cow-milking contest. This contest—it goes like this.

"We set up two-man teams to compete against one another. Then we cut as many cows from the herd as we have teams. Then the man in charge—that's going to be Mickey O'Rourke— he gives a signal and the first two-man team goes running after one of the cows from the cut.

"One member of the team grabs hold of the cow—if he can catch it—by the head. He holds onto it—if he can. Meanwhile— are you following me, Wes—the other man on the team—he's got a tin can in his hand and it's up to him to milk the cow his partner's hanging onto and run back to the finish line—that's where Mickey O'Rourke will be standing. The team that gets their can of milk back to the finish line the fastest—they're the winners."

"You were right, Slim," Bannock said with a wry smile. "Barney does come up with some pretty crazy ideas."

"You don't want to compete, Mr. Bannock?" Slim asked.

"Sure, I do," Bannock responded without hesitation. "I've

never been a man who walked away from a challenge, not even a crazy one like this."

"How about you, Wes?" Slim prompted.

The foreman nodded. "I'm in."

"Pick your partners, then," Slim advised. "I'm already paired with Ed Rambleau."

"Viviano!" Bannock called out as Wes headed for the campfire and the group of men standing around it. "Come on over here!"

The Mexican Bannock had summoned arrived on the run and skidded to a halt. "You want me, boss?"

"I do, Viviano. You've heard about the cow-milking contest?"

Viviano nodded and broke into a toothy grin. "Another one of Barney's loco ideas. *Sí,* I have heard of it."

"How'd you like to be my partner? I know you're one of the fastest runners I've got working on the ranch. I still remember the time we were all up in Abilene at the end of a drive and we got a little rambunctious—drunk is the word—and the law came down on us and you went running out of town on foot and back to the herd as if the devil himself was on your backtrail. That Abilene law dog threw the rest of us in jail overnight that time but he never did get his hands on you."

Viviano did the impossible. He grinned even more widely. "You and me, boss, we show these ranch hands how to win this cow-milking contest."

"Let's go," Bannock said, clapping an arm around Viviano's shoulder. "It looks like they're getting ready to begin."

He and the Mexican ranch hand made their way over to where Mickey O'Rourke was giving last minute instructions on the rules of the contest to the assembled contestants—a total of three teams of two men each.

"Any of you buckaroos wind up back over the finish line without any milk in your can you're disqualified, got that? So is any team that interferes with any other team, wittingly or unwittingly. This contest is being run fair and square and altogether aboveboard."

"You're all set, are you?" Bannock asked Wes, who had teamed up with a rawboned cowboy named Rusty.

"We're ready, boss," Rusty declared, rubbing his hands together.

"As ready as we're ever going to be," Wes added.

"You and Viviano are going to compete, I take it," Rusty observed.

"Yep," Bannock said. "It's going to be Viviano Colorado and Ben Bannock against the world."

"All right, gents," intoned Mickey O'Rourke as he took a Waltham watch from a vest pocket and snapped it open. "Who will go first?"

Slim and Ed Rambleau both put a hand up into the air.

"Very good, lads," O'Rourke said. Then, shouting, "Wade, will you do these fine broths of boys a favor and cut a cow out of the herd for them to go after?"

Wade, who was astride a buckskin, wheeled his mount and headed for the herd. Minutes later, he had cut a cow out of it and chased the animal out into the open.

"On your mark!" O'Rourke cried, squinting at his watch. "*Go!*"

Slim and Ed went racing toward the cow, which was already on her way back to the herd and the security she knew she would feel there.

Ed cut her off. Then, without a moment's hesitation, he jumped at her and clasped her head in both arms. She shuddered and shook but Ed maintained his hold, keeping the cow's face pressed against his broad chest so that she could not see.

As Slim hunkered down behind beside the cow and seized a teat, cheers from some of the onlookers went up. Pulling and squeezing on the cow's teat, Slim sent milk squirting into the tin can he had been given by the cook.

"Come on, Slim," someone shouted and Slim, as if responding to the cry, straightened. Holding the can containing the milk out in front of him with both hands, he began to sprint toward the finish line.

Behind him, his partner, Ed, released the cow, which went bawling in injured innocence back to the herd.

"Four minutes and fifty-one seconds!" declared O'Rourke as Slim crossed the finish line, milk sloshing out of the can in his hands as he did so.

"Beat that, boys!" he exulted as Ed joined him and both men congratulated one another on their time.

"Next!" O'Rourke called out.

Viviano Colorado took a step toward the finish line but Bannock reached out and drew him back.

"Let's go last," Bannock suggested. "That way, we'll know what the competition's done and what times we have to beat to win."

Wes Holbrook and Rusty stepped up to the finish line, bent over, their hands on their knees, their heels dug in as they waited for the signal to head for the second cow the cowboy named Wade had cut from the herd for them.

"On your mark," O'Rourke cried. "Get set. Go!"

Wes and Dusty headed straight for the cow that stood still, seemingly confused, as they neared her. Then, tossing her head, she turned and fled from them.

"Get her!" Wes yelled to Rusty.

Rusty tried but the cow managed to evade him by making a sharp turn to the right. He skidded to a halt, turned and went after the running cow. She bawled in distress and turned sharply to the left. Again she eluded Rusty.

But now Wes, who had anticipated her maneuver, had come up on her left flank so that she almost collided with him when she made her turn. He threw his arms around her neck while skidding along the ground, his boots raising a cloud of dust that made both him and the cow he had captured cough.

Rusty dropped to his knees and seized a teat. Milk splatted into the can in his hand.

"That's enough!" Wes yelled. "Head for the finish line!"

Rusty obediently did, holding the can above his head in one steady hand.

"Four minutes and two seconds!" O'Rourke cried for all to hear as Rusty crossed the finish line with Wes right behind him.

The partners clapped one another on the back and then turned expectant smiles on Bannock and Viviano.

"With all due respect, boss," Wes said, "I don't think you have a chance of beating our time."

"We'll see about that," Bannock said mildly as he watched Wade cut a third cow out of the herd.

"Now then, me boyos, be you both ready for the fray?" O'Rourke inquired, glancing from his watch to Bannock and Viviano.

"*Sí,*" said Viviano without taking his eyes from the lone cow in the distance.

"Yes," said Bannock, tightly gripping the empty can in his hands.

"On your marks!" O'Rourke shouted. "Get set. *Go!*"

Bannock and Viviano went. Like the wind. Both men raced toward the cow that was ambling back toward the herd in the distance. Viviano was the first to reach the animal. As she shied from him, he reached out and caught her in a firm head-lock. She promptly pulled away, dragging Viviano along with her.

"Hold her still!" Bannock yelled as he bent down and tried for a second time to seize a teat.

But the cow pulled away again and this time managed to break free of Viviano, who, cursing, went right after her and once again got an arm around her neck. When the cow tried again to free herself, Viviano used his free hand to twist her ear.

The cow bawled in protest of the pain. And then tried once more to escape.

Viviano twisted her ear.

The cow responded by staying put.

Viviano let go of her ear.

"Got it!" Bannock yelled and straightened up.

The cow chose that moment to kick out with her hind legs. They knocked the can that was half full of milk from Bannock's hand.

"Damnation!" he muttered. He retrieved the can, bent down and, watching warily in case the cow decided to kick again, resumed milking. This time he quit when he had a quarter can full of milk. He went racing toward the finish line, the milk sloshing out of the can he was carrying.

But not all the milk sloshed out of the can. There was enough left in the can when Bannock crossed the finish line to satisfy O'Rourke, who, as a breathless Viviano came dashing up to him and Bannock, announced, "Three minutes and fifty-nine seconds!"

Cheers went up from the assembled ranch hands.

"I hereby declare these two boyos to be the winners of the official Bannock ranch cow-milking contest and will brook no argument or sass from any man about my declaration," O'Rourke declared expansively.

"Three seconds," Wes Holbrook muttered, looking glum. "Rusty and me lost by three lousy seconds." Then, brightening, he shook Bannock's hand and then Viviano's. "The best men won," he declared.

"But only by a mere three seconds," Bannock reminded him. "If it hadn't been for Viviano, we would have lost for certain. Did you see the way I let that cow kick the can out of my hand?"

"Nevertheless, you won," Wes said, and added, "I bet on me and Rusty to win so I owe Wade four bits."

"We show them how to win a contest, boss, no?"

As Wes left to pay his debt to Wade, Bannock turned to Viviano and said, "We sure did. We make quite a team, Viviano. Why, with my speed and your brains, there's no telling how many contests we might win in days to come."

A pause and then, "Tell me something, Viviano. I was pretty busy trying to milk that cow so I didn't see—how'd you manage to hang on to the critter the way you did?"

Viviano grinned and melodramatically stroked his droopy black mustache with both work-worn hands. "I tell the lady I am mucho in love with her. We are now—how you say it—engaged?"

Bannock couldn't help himself. He burst into uproarious laughter. "Viviano, should you hear of any more such contests, just call my name and I'll come a'running with my hat throwed back and my spurs a'jingling."

"*Sí*, I will do that, boss. I make you the promise."

Bannock went over to where Wes was standing alone near the chuck wagon. "I think I'll mosey on now."

"You're heading back to the ranch?"

"I'll be stopping there to get my gun and then I'm planning on heading south to pay Phil McIntyre a visit. I think it's high time—past time, as a matter of fact—that him and me had ourselves a little talk about how his calves have gotten into the bad habit of sucking cows bearing the Double B brand."

"You're expecting to need your gun when you go up against McIntyre?" Wes asked, frowning. "You're figuring that hot words will lead to hot lead?"

Bannock shook his head. "I don't expect to have to use my gun on McIntyre. But these days when a man heads south toward the border it seems to me he ought to go armed. Be seeing you, Wes."

Bannock left the foreman and went over to the makeshift corral the wrangler had strung among some post oak trees downwind of the camp.

He brought his blood bay out of the enclosure and then saddled and bridled it. Flipping down his stirrups after making sure his cinch was tight, he swung into the saddle and rode out of the cow camp, giving a wave to Wes as he went.

Later as he crested a low hill and his ranch house and outbuildings came into view, Bannock felt the familiar thrill that the homeplace always brought him. It was a feeling composed of unequal parts of pride, a sense of place, a feeling of security and not a little love.

The house itself was built of stone which had a faintly pink cast to it when the sun struck it. It was two stories high, square, with stone chimneys on either end of it. Fronting it was a veranda edged with a low stone wall from which wooden pillars rose to support a shingled overhang. Locust trees shaded it in front and on the north where they formed a windbreak.

Some distance from the house was a barn, painted red and imposing in its size. Next to the barn was an adobe tack house and some distance away sprawled the long rectangular bunkhouse with a boardwalk fronting it and an overhang supported by stout timbers.

A three-sided shed facing south contained neatly stacked cords of wood and beyond it was a stone well. The corral was man-high and located behind the house. A pole snake fence with a swinging gate set in it surrounded the main house.

Bannock drew rein in front of the house and, leaving his bay ground-hitched, went inside into the relatively cool interior of the living room. Heavy leather furniture filled it. A bright red and blue woven Navajo rug covered most of the puncheon floor. There was a gilt-framed mirror on the wall facing the front door and shelves holding books lined one side wall. Small wooden tables supporting lamps were scattered about the living room. Through the windows that lined the wall on both sides of the door light streamed.

Bannock went to his gun rack, unlocked it and took from it a Henry rifle. From a table, he picked up his cartridge belt. A Navy Colt occupied its holster. He strapped it around his waist, adjusting it until it hung just right and was within easy reach of his right hand. He drew the revolver and checked to make sure it was loaded. It was, with its hammer resting on an empty chamber.

He left the house and stepped into the saddle again. Turning his horse, he headed south, passing on the way a gleaming new barbed wire fence that belonged to the Peterson spread. His eyes left it and roved over the unfenced land opposite it. The presence of the fence rankled within him. Bannock was not a man who could easily abide fences, or barriers of any kind for that matter. Bannock was a man who preferred—needed—open spaces and the freedom they represented. Fences were meant to keep people out—or in. They always seemed to challenge Bannock and he had to make a conscious effort to hide the deep resentment they aroused in him.

Clouds—fat, fluffy and white—drifted in the sky above him. The land stretched, seemingly without end, all around him as did the sky. To his right was a low ragged range of hills. On his left, a stream wound like a ribbon carelessly dropped upon the land. It sparkled in the sunlight. The feeling of contentment— the feeling that all was right with the world—that Bannock always gained from riding across open range gradually gave way, as he came closer to his destination, to a distinct feeling of unease that was only partially alleviated by the comforting weight of the gun on his hip.

He rode on but before he had reached his destination he heard the sound of a shot fired in the distance. It was followed by the sound of pounding hooves. Bannock was sure that what he was hearing was not the sound of horses coming his way. Based on the loudness of the sound and its rhythm, he was almost positive it was cattle.

A stampede?

He drew rein and sat his saddle, watching and listening. He heard another shot. The ground-pounding sound grew even louder. Then the first of what would become a small herd of cattle, a mossy-horned steer leading them, rounded a bend up ahead of Bannock and came hurtling toward him.

He slammed his spurs into his bay's flanks and the animal broke into a fast trot that quickly became a gallop. Once he was safely out of the path of the advancing herd that was stirring up thick clouds of dust, Bannock looked back at them, trying to determine what it was that was driving them, wondering what it was that had spooked them.

He had the answers to his questions within seconds. Two men, both of them Mexicans, rode into sight behind the herd. They had six-guns in their hands and one of the men fired a shot as he rode hell-for-leather behind the stampeding herd. The other man laughed and flailed with a coiled rope at the rumps of the animals bringing up the rear, forcing them to move faster.

Two more rounds, fired in quick succession, sounded. Bannock knew neither had been fired by the Mexicans. There must, he reasoned, be other rustlers around. He was convinced that he was witnessing an attempt to steal cattle by the Mexicans who had obviously stampeded the herd. Although he couldn't make out the brands the cattle carried because of their distance from him and the thick dust they had raised which swirled around them, he was willing to bet they were some—maybe all—of Tom Butler's stock.

He spurred his horse and rode back the way he had come. Then he angled to the left and headed straight for the lead steer. As he did so, he saw two more riders rounding the bend in the distance. He recognized Tom Butler and one of Tom's hands whose face was familiar but whose name he couldn't recall.

He rode on, bent low over his horse's neck, gripping the reins with his left hand, his right hand going for his gun.

When the Mexicans saw him coming, they both rode out from behind the herd and headed for him. Behind them, Butler and his hired hand headed for them.

When Bannock came within ten yards of the lead steer, he fired a round that bit into the ground directly in front of the animal's flying front feet.

It caused the mossy horn's head and horns to jerk up and back. But it didn't stop the animal or the cattle crowding up so close behind it.

But Bannock's second round stopped the lead steer when it burned its way into the animal's brain.

The steer went down with its right front leg raised and ready to take its next step. A few of the animals behind it stumbled over the corpse. Others tried to avoid it, swerving to the right and to the left.

Bannock rode on past the steer he had dropped and out of the way of the herd that was rapidly losing its sense of direction now that its leader was dead. He wheeled his horse around and looked back. The stampede was dissolving into what he was sure would, in a matter of just a few more minutes, become nothing more dangerous than a mill.

His attention was diverted from the cattle to Butler as the cattleman fired a shot at one of the Mexicans that missed. Butler's target, a swarthy man with a thick mustache, flared nostrils and a livid scar that ran across his forehead just above his crow-black eyes, stood up in his saddle and returned Butler's fire. Then he squeezed off a shot that went whining uncomfortably close to Bannock's right ear and sent him riding hard and fast in search of some kind of cover.

THREE

THE WOODS!

Bannock headed for them, cat-tracking his bay with his spurs in his haste to escape the rounds the Mexicans were firing at him as he fled.

His flight ended as he rode in among a scraggly stand of sycamores and leaped from the saddle to crouch, gun gripped tightly in both hands, behind the trunk of one of the trees. He had no sooner done so when a round screamed toward him. It struck the tree trunk, sending fragments of bark flying into his face. He pulled back behind the tree, his back pressing against it, as he tried to make of himself as small a target as possible.

Another round whined past him, hitting neither him nor the trunk of the tree that was serving him as a makeshift breastwork. When no others followed it, he peered cautiously around the tree.

The Mexicans were down behind some frost-cracked boulders, only the guns in their hands showing as they fired at Tom Butler and the man with him who had taken cover behind some of the cattle that had formed a small cluster which was slowly milling in the distance. As Bannock took aim at the Mexican marauders—what little he could see of them—a steer bawled and went down, hit by one of the pair. It lay convulsing on the

ground and losing blood in rhythmic spurts as its heart pumped
the fluid out of the wound in its chest onto the ground.

Bannock squeezed off a round which had the effect of making
the two guns disappear behind the boulders.

"I'm going to kill you goddam greasers!" the man with Butler
shouted—the sound almost a demented scream. He fired. Once.
Twice.

Shards of stone flew up into the air from the boulder behind
which the Mexicans were pinned down as were Bannock and the
other two ranchers in their respective positions.

Bannock rose and, holding his breath, ran through the trees
to take up a new position some distance away behind a deadfall
propped at a forty-five-degree angle against a living sycamore.
He fired a shot and then swiftly thumbed cartridges out of his
belt and filled the empty chambers of his revolver.

His fire was returned by one of the Mexicans.

Bannock grunted with satisfaction. From his new and deliberately chosen position, he had managed to split the attention of
the two men behind the boulders. One of them now had to
attend to Butler and the man with him while the other one had
to keep Bannock in his sights. His calculated move thus had the
effect of halving the firepower available to the Mexicans to use
on the two points from which they were being attacked.

Bannock fired again and hit the boulder which he had aimed
at. He heard the faint sound of angry Spanish being spat into
the air.

"Fuego!"

Both Mexicans did fire then, their shots shattering dry limbs
of the deadfall behind which Bannock still crouched. He got up
and, staying low, ran deeper into the woods. Behind him, another round plowed into the deadfall. He ran on.

Someone screamed.

Bannock, the trees flashing past him as he continued running,
looked back over his shoulder. But he could not see who had
been hit. Someone had, he knew. No other reason for that

agonized scream. Had it been one of the Mexicans? Butler? The man with him?

He halted at the edge of the woods and stood behind a tree, not a muscle in his body moving as he surveyed the scene from his new vantage point. No fire was coming from Butler's position. A bad sign. He could see the backs of the Mexicans now because he had circled around behind them.

The one with the scar on his forehead, the one who had fired at him earlier and almost taken off his ear, was aiming at the deadfall where Bannock had been. The man with him had his gun trained on Butler's position. Neither man appeared to have been wounded.

Which meant that either Butler or the ranch hand with him had been hit and had screamed. Gritting his teeth, Bannock moved out of the trees into the open. He loped toward the Mexicans, tracing a path through thick grass so that it would muffle his footsteps to some degree.

But the Mexicans heard him coming nevertheless. Both of them turned and, still crouching, fired at him. An instant before flames flew from the muzzles of their revolvers, Bannock had thrown himself to the ground where he lay prone as he fired snap shots at his attackers. He got one of them with his first round.

The man, a look of pained surprise twisting his features, shot to his feet. His hands rose. He dropped his gun as he slammed back against the boulder behind him. He looked down at the small red hole in his chest as he slid slowly down the boulder. He crumbled to the ground in a heap, a bloody streak staining the boulder from Bannock's bullet's exit wound in his back.

His companion, the man with the scar, shouted, *"Vamos!"* Then, as he leaped to his feet, he saw his companion lying behind him and knew that the man was not going anywhere. He ran to his horse and bounded into the saddle, getting off a final shot at Bannock, who got up on one knee and sent a round whining his way.

It missed the Mexican, who wheeled his horse and went galloping away. Bannock fired again, a parting shot which also missed.

He turned and circled the milling cattle. Once past them, he found Tom Butler down on his knees on the ground beside the inert body of the man who had been with him. Butler looked up as Bannock approached, a stricken expression on his weather-worn face.

"They killed him, Ben," he said, his voice shaky. "The bastards killed Josh."

Josh. Bannock remembered the man's name now. Josh Cameron. A good ranch hand. One of the best. He had met the man the previous year when Butler had held a dance for neighboring ranchers following the fall roundup.

"What happened, Tom?" Bannock asked.

Slowly, Butler rose to his feet and stood there, a forlorn figure, staring down at the body lying by his boots. "Josh and I, we were roaming around out here hunting strays. We'd found that bunch"—he pointed to the milling cattle—"and were driving them back to the ranch when those two greasers came by and threw down on us before the howdys were even over. They wanted our cows and they got them. I was ready to let them have them but Josh—well, Josh has—had—himself one helluva hot temper. He said I could do as I damn well please but he wasn't going to stand still for them making off with our stock. He was going after them and he meant to get the cattle back.

"I tried at first to talk him out of it but it weren't no use. Josh was bound and determined. I told him we could get ourselves killed if we went after those greasers and I, for one, didn't want to die. I know you think I'm a coward, Ben—"

"I don't think any such thing, Tom."

"I'm a cattleman, Ben, not a gunfighter. I didn't fancy losing my cows to thieves but neither did I want to try to get them back at the price of my life."

"I understand, Tom. None of us around here are gunhawks. But I'll tell you this. It's beginning to look to me like we're all going to have to learn how to be such if we're to keep what's ours and stay alive into the bargain."

Butler nodded mutely. Then, "This whole damned thing started back in the winter of '64."

"I lost close to a hundred head that winter. They froze to death standing in snow up to their spines."

"Everybody's cattle started drifting south trying to get away from that winter. It weren't long before the greasers down in Old Mexico spotted them and just took them for their own. Those strays were a bonanza for them. Now that they've developed an appetite for the cattle business, they're getting more mean by the minute. Though they never did come this far north before, far as I know."

"The thing that gets me about all this, Tom, is that those border ruffians are claiming that they're not doing anything wrong. That they're just taking what's rightfully theirs in the first place since everything between the Nueces River and the Rio Bravo was theirs to begin with. So they claim they're just taking back what rightfully belongs to them anyway."

"That's like a little kid stealing cookies out of his mama's jar and saying he couldn't help it 'cuz he was powerful hungry."

"I hear Colonel Mantavo's been stocking his ranch down at Matamoros with Texas cattle—those that are left after he sells off some to other ranches in Mexico."

"The Commander of the Line of the Bravo's a slick customer, no doubt about it. I hear he was a good soldier during the war and the government down there thinks he's some kind of saint as a result and won't lift a finger to hinder his pillaging and plundering. Why, I read in the paper the other day that some say close to a hundred thousand head have been stolen by Mantavo and his men. That's not to mention the awful things those dirty greasers have done to innocent men and women and even children. You heard about Phil McIntyre, didn't you, Ben?"

"I was just on my way to pay McIntyre a visit when I ran into the ruckus you were having with those Mexicans. What happened to McIntyre?"

"They killed him, Ben, him and his missus both."

"They? You mean Mantavo's border bandits?"

"The very same. From what I hear, McIntyre came upon them trying to run cattle off his range while him and his missus were driving back from town. McIntyre was still alive when he was found—just barely—and he said it was Mantavo himself who had put a knife into him. His feet were nearly burned off. What was worse, he said they ravaged Amelia McIntyre before they killed her. They made McIntyre watch the whole evil thing, Ben."

Bannock was shocked. Stunned. He had not heard the news and now that he had, his stomach was sinking and his gorge was rising.

"It's bad, Ben," Butler said solemnly, looking down again at Cameron's corpse. "It's bad and getting worse. If the damned Reconstructionists hadn't of went and disbanded the Texas Rangers we'd have some protection. But, as things stand, we're like sheep just waiting for the shearing."

"We've got to fight back one way or another, Tom."

"That's all well and good for you to say, Ben. You've got a big spread and lots of men working it. Me, I've got just myself, my boy Billy and Josh. I mean I *had* Josh. Hell, things have been moving so fast and furious around here of late, that my mind keeps getting muddled. You've got the means with which to fight back. I don't."

"What we ought to do maybe is band together into some kind of organization."

"There's already been some talk along those lines. You know that new fellow, Bob Pace, that came down here from Kansas last month?"

"I've heard his name bandied about but I've not met him as yet."

"Well, Pace is talking about getting a group of stockmen together and going after Mantavo and his men. He says the greasers that are living around here probably know what's going on where those border bandits are concerned. They probably know, Pace says, when and where Mantavo is going to make his next move. He says we could get hold of one or two of those fellows and get them to keep us informed. Pace says if they won't cooperate, we can try Mantavo's own tactics on them."

"This fellow Pace is talking torture?"

"He calls it 'persuasion.'"

Bannock shook his head. "That's not my cup of tea, Tom. I don't hold with such shenanigans whether they come from men on the south or the north side of the border."

"That's all well and good for you to say but some of us don't have the manpower or other wherewithal to take a stand against those greasers. It's easy for you to talk pious and preacherish about what you do and don't hold with."

"Now, just hold on a damn minute, Tom. I'm not sounding pious or preacherish. I certainly don't mean to sound that way. I was just expressing an opinion. I wasn't trying to sell it to anybody, especially not to you."

"Look here, Ben—" Tom began, bristling, and angrily shaking a finger in Bannock's face.

He stopped speaking in mid-sentence. He sighed and shook his head. "Listen to me, will you? This damned state of affairs has got two old-time friends tearing at each other's throats like dogs made mad by the summer sun. I'm sorry, Ben. I never should have jumped on you the way I just did."

"Tom, have you thought about hiring some extra hands? Just until this storm blows over? To help you look after your stock and homestead, I mean."

"I've thought about it. But hired hands cost cash money and most of my money's tied up in my cattle and crops, Ben. I've got none to use to pay hired guns."

"Are you going to hook up with Bob Pace and be a vigilante like he's advocating?"

"I don't know what the hell I'm going to do," Butler declared with bitterness in his voice. "I guess the first thing I'm going to do is arrange for the burying of Josh there."

Bannock looked down at the body lying on the ground. Then he helped Butler lift it and carry it over to Cameron's horse. The two men draped it over the animal's saddle, arms and legs hanging limply down on either side, and then Bannock stood by as Butler got his own horse and boarded it.

"Wait a minute, Tom," he said. "I'll be right back." He went to where he had left his horse and began to lead it back to where Butler was sitting his saddle and watching him. On the way, he picked up the reins of the horse that belonged to the Mexican he had shot and killed.

"You might as well take this horse along home with you," he told Butler when he reached the rancher. He handed up the reins. "The man who owned it won't be needing it anymore. Consider it found stock."

"Will you be coming by for the burying, Ben?"

"I'll be there. What time will it be?"

"Some time tomorrow. Say three o'clock in the afternoon. First I've got to go into town and buy a box to put Josh in and then I've got to get the bad news out to his friends. I'll send my boy, Billy, to spread the word.

"I'll see you then, Tom."

At three-thirty the next afternoon Bannock stood, hat in hand and head bowed, beside an open grave under a willow tree a half mile from the Butler ranch house.

On planks laid across the grave rested a pine coffin that was nailed shut. Ropes ran under it to each side of the grave where the mourners stood.

Billy Butler and his father. Kate Butler. A few hands from neighboring ranches who had known and worked roundups with Josh Cameron. A preacher with a fringe of gray hair and mournful eyes that matched the tone of his voice.

In the black-clad man's hand was a worn leather-bound Bible. He raised his eyes to the sky and said, "We are gathered here this sad day to bid farewell to a friend and colleague, dearly beloved. Josh Cameron, the fallen, was the victim of evil forces abroad in the world. *Evil* forces, I say!"

The preacher slammed a fist down on his Bible and his fiery eyes roamed from face to face. "As true Christian believers, we cannot raise our voices in calls for vengeance. No, dearly beloved, vengeance is mine saith the Lord. And yet"—the preacher's eyes squeezed shut and his jowls trembled—"and yet," he repeated, his eyes still closed, "our hearts ache and our spirits shrivel in the face of this dastardly deed that has laid low our brother, Joshua. Our voices cry out, if not for vengeance, then at least for understanding.

"*But,* dearly beloved, when understanding comes, as it has to each of us, then our hands can do nothing but form fists with which to strike man's and God's enemies. Our voices must be raised not only in protest but in denunciation. I say, *dee—nun—cee—ay—shun,* dearly beloved!"

The preacher's eyes snapped open. There was rage roaming in them. "We must act, dearly beloved, to prevent what has happened to Joshua Cameron from happening to the rest of us and to those dear to us. We must take up the cudgels of the Lord Almighty and strike our blows for peace and harmony under God's great sky so that no more blood may be shed and no more tears need be wept for the dear departed.

"For my text today, I have chosen Psalm Fifty-six because I believe it to be appropriate and fitting for this melancholy occasion."

The preacher opened his Bible to the page marked by a red ribbon.

"This psalm, dearly beloved, is to the chief Musician upon Jonath-elemrechokim, Michtam of David, when the Philistines took him to Gath.

Be merciful unto me, O God: for man would swallow me up;
  he fighting daily oppresseth me.

Mine enemies would daily swallow me up: for they be many
    that fight against me, O thou most High.
What time I am afraid, I will trust in thee.
In God I will praise his word, in God I have put my trust;
    I will not fear what flesh can do unto me.
Every day they wrest my words: all their thoughts are
    against me for evil.

As the preacher continued reading the psalm, Bannock heard
not holy words but a war cry. A war cry for the vengeance the
preacher had earlier seemed to reject. He looked up at the man.
The preacher's pale cheeks had become flushed.

Bannock could see the anger in the eyes of the other mourners. Their expressions were grim; their jaws set. Keep it up, he
thought, as he returned his gaze to the loudly reading preacher,
and you'll have another Crusade on your hands. Anglos against
Mexicans. Then blood won't only flow; it'll flood this land of
ours.

In God have I put my trust: I will not be afraid
    what man can do unto me.
Thy vows are upon me, O God: I will render praises
    unto thee.
For thou hast delivered my soul from death: wilt not
    thou deliver my feet from falling, that I may walk
    before God in the light of the living?

The preacher clapped shut his Bible and raised his eyes to
heaven. "Hallelujah," he said, almost in a whisper. And then,
shouting: *"Hallelujah* and amen, Lord God Almighty!"

A chorus of "amens" echoed the preacher, who nodded to
the men standing on either side of the grave.

They removed the planks, picked up the ropes and slowly
lowered the coffin into the ground.

"May the seraphim and cherubim welcome thee with open
arms," the preacher intoned, "and may they escort thee rejoic-
ing into the awesome presence of thy living God." He picked up

a handful of dirt and tossed it down upon the coffin resting in its grave.

Then, as the preacher left the gravesite, Bannock waited until the small crowd of people gathered around the Butlers had thinned out before going over to Tom Butler and offering his hand.

"Josh Cameron was a fine man," he said as the two men shook hands. "You'll miss him, Tom."

"That I will."

"Hello, Kate," Bannock said. "Billy."

"It was good of you to come, Ben," Kate said. "Thank you."

"Why don't you and the boy go up to the house, Kate," Butler suggested. "I want to have a word with Ben."

When his wife and son had gone, Butler said, "Josh isn't all I'm going to miss, Ben. I'm going to miss you too. You've been a staunch friend to me in both good times and bad."

"What are you talking about, Tom?"

"Last night Kate and I—Billy too—we talked things over. We're leaving, Ben."

"Leaving?"

"We're heading north. Kate's got a sister up in San Antonio. We'll light there for a spell until I can figure out what to do next. What I wanted to talk to you about, Ben, was would you be interested in buying my stock from me?"

"Well, I—well, yes, I guess I would. But—Tom, are you sure you're doing the right thing, making the right move? This trouble we've been having—it can't last forever and you've built up a fine spread here. I'm not at all sure a dyed-in-the-wool cattleman like you'll be happy in a city the size of San Antonio."

"You may be right. I have an unhappy inkling that you are. But the fact remains, we're going. Like I said, we talked it all over. We turned it this way and we turned it that way. After worrying the matter half to death we all came to the same conclusion. Things are getting too dangerous around here to suit us. Ben, I've got to think of Kate and the boy. If anything happened to me the way it did to Josh—well, nobody'd take much note of losing an old curmudgeon like me except for my wife and son, of course. But I can't stand by and let anything happen to either one of them, now can I?"

Bannock put his hat on and pulled it down low on his forehead to shield his eyes from the sun. "No, I guess, you can't. Put that way, I can see why you have to do what you say you're fixing to do. But I sure do hate to see you go. I'm not a sentimental sort but I have to say I'll sorely miss you all. When do you plan to leave?"

"Just as soon as I can sell my stock and homeplace. Which brings us right back to the matter at hand. How much would you be willing to pay for my cows, Ben? I've got close to four hundred head as of the spring increase."

Bannock made Butler an offer, expecting the usual quibbling and bargaining over it, but to his surprise Butler accepted it with alacrity.

"I appreciate the fairness of your offer, Ben," the rancher said. "It's not just fair; it's downright generous. Will you send some of your hands over to drive the stock onto your range?"

"When do you want me to send them?"

"Soon as you can. Now that I've made up my mind I'm anxious to make my move." A pause and then, "Ben, you don't think maybe you and your boys ought to light a shuck? Just till the bad storm we're having blows over?"

Bannock shook his head. "We'll stay and try our best to weather it. I'll send Wes over first thing in the morning with a draft in the amount we've agreed on for your cattle. He'll bring some of the boys and they'll drive your stock onto my range."

Butler started to say something, seemed to think better of it and held out his hand.

Bannock shook it and then they parted, Butler trudging toward his homestead and Bannock heading for his horse, which he'd left ground-hitched in the midst of some good browse growing out of the sun. When he reached it, he swung into the saddle and sat there for a moment, hands wrapped around his saddle horn, and watched the men who had lowered Josh

Cameron's coffin into its grave as they shoveled dirt down upon
it. He could hear the faint thuds clods of earth were making as
they struck the pine box. He was reminded of another funeral,
one that had taken place years ago, one at which he had openly
wept, unable to contain his overwhelming grief.

Her name had been Nora. Nora Soames until she became
Mrs. Ben Bannock. She had been a pretty little thing, "soft as a
calf's ear," Bannock had told her more than once in a teasing
fashion. She had made a daily miracle of the world; her laughter
was the sound of delight and joy.

He had, quite simply, adored her. It was because of her and
his love for her that he had been able, he was convinced, to build
the homestead he now lived in alone and lonely and to manage
his herd until it had grown to rival the best in Texas. He saw her
now in his mind's eye—her long brown hair shining and her
blue eyes dancing. He saw her heart-shaped face and the dimple
in her chin that he swore at times actually twinkled. He saw her
lean and lithe figure, her provocative hips, the sweet curve of
her lovely young breasts. She glowed in his memory. She
gleamed.

There she was, running across a summer meadow, straw hat,
red-beribboned, in her hand. And there—stringing cranberries
and popcorn to make decorative garlands for their Christmas
tree. Opening her warm arms to welcome him, as always, to the
tenderness and comfort of the marriage bed they shared.

She died in the spring when everything else in the world was
coming alive. But it would have been as bad for him had she
died when January lay burdened with snow and ice. Pleurisy, the
doctor said. Her loss was a knife in his heart. The wound it left
had only now begun to heal.

He swallowed hard. Blinked the wetness from his eyes.
Turned his horse and headed for home.

He forced himself to think of nothing as he rode, guiding his
bay with knee pressure alone. The horse maintained a steady
trot, the sound of its hooves striking the ground rhythmic and
somehow reassuring to Bannock. Proof, he supposed, that the

world went on and those in it, though crushed by grief, were forced, in the bitter end, to do the same.

The bay slowed its pace as it began to climb a hill. It snorted, its breath coming in short sharp gusts. Absentmindedly, Bannock reached out and stroked its slightly sweaty neck. The horse fell silent and, as if encouraged by his gesture, increased its pace. Bannock shifted his weight to make the climb easier for the animal, pulling his feet out of the stirrups and letting them dangle.

As he crested the hill and started down the other side, he saw them. Tom Butler's cattle. They were spread out across a rolling prairie thick with grama grass and buttercups in bright yellow bloom. A wide stream cut through the tableland, glistening in the sun.

No, he thought as he rode toward them. They're not Tom's anymore. Now they're mine.

Before he reached the bottom of the hill, the riders appeared. Four of them came bursting out of a ragged stand of blackjack oaks far to the west, lashing their horses with their reins.

Mexicans. All armed.

Bannock stiffened and drew rein, his hand dropping to the butt of his revolver.

The men seemed not to be aware of his presence as they rode straight toward a pair of cows which were lying down on the ground, their heads moving indolently from side to side as they contentedly chewed their cuds.

Rustlers!

Bannock surveyed the immediate area, looking for someplace, some strategic place, from which he could go up against the four men. A foolish idea, with the odds four-to-one? Maybe. But he'd be damned if he'd let them make off with any of his stock.

There was no time to ride back and get Tom and Billy Butler to come to his aid. And he was too far from his own spread to ride there for help. In both cases, by the time he got back with

men siding him the rustlers would be long gone and so would
the stock he had just arranged to buy from Butler.

His eyes fell on a dry gulch cut into the land where once a
stream had flowed. He wheeled his bay and headed for it. If he
could get there in time—if he could get there before the rustlers
spotted him . . .

He slid down the side of his horse, holding tightly to the
saddle horn with both hands, one foot hooked around the cantle
of his saddle. He rode that way, Indian warrior fashion, until he
reached the gully, keeping out of sight of the four Mexicans in
the far distance. If they had looked his way, they would, he
hoped, have thought they were seeing nothing more threatening than somebody's runaway mount.

At the gully, he drew rein and brought his bay to a sudden
stop. The horse's head jerked back as the bit grew tight in its
mouth. Bannock let himself drop to the ground. As his horse
wandered a few steps, he bellied his way down into the dusty
gully. There he took off his hat, drew his revolver, took aim and
stared in disbelief at what he was seeing. While he had been
riding hard for the shelter of the gully, the four men had not
rustled so much as a single cow. What they *had* done was rouse
the two cows that had been lying down and they were now
pursuing them as both animals ran bawling in fright.

The knives they had in their hands, Bannock saw, were not
ordinary knives but the wicked get-the-guts knives—the *media
luna*—of Mexican hide-peelers, the weapons that looked more
like scythes than ordinary knives.

One of the four men moved in at a sharp angle toward the cow
that was trailing her companion. He leaned down toward the
animal and the knife in his hand glinted in the sun as he slashed
at the animal. He missed on his first try but he achieved his
purpose on his second try. He managed to hamstring the cow
with his half-moon-shaped knife that was mounted on a long
shaft.

The cow went down and rolled over, blood spraying from her
wounded hind leg. She immediately struggled back to her feet

and tried to run but the man opposite the one who had downed her swung his deadly blade and cut the tendons in her other hind leg. This time when the cow went down and tried again to rise in order to escape her tormentors, she could raise only her front legs. Her hind legs remained helpless on the ground, unable to support her hindquarters.

The other two Mexicans who had been riding just behind the men who had hamstrung the cow moved up as their companions rode off after the second cow. They leaped from their saddles and, using bowie knives, began to skin the helpless cow—skin her alive.

Bannock, watching, winced as the cow bawled and her great eyes rolled in terror and absolute agony. She tried to drag herself along the ground to get away but could not after one of the Mexicans raised a booted foot and slammed it violently down upon the back of her neck, pinning her to the bloody ground beneath her.

The skinning proceeded apace as the other two hide-peelers repeated what they had just done to the other cow that had initially failed to escape from them.

Bannock, cursing volubly, thumbed back the hammer of his gun and squeezed off a round. His cursing continued when his shot plowed as planned, not into either of the two hide-peeling Mexicans, but into the body of the cow they were stripping of her hide while she still lived and struggled in vain to escape from them.

The two Mexicans straightened and drew their guns. Both of them turned in circles, searching for the spot from which the round had come—and for the one who had fired it. Bannock's finger tightened on the trigger and then he sent another shot screaming toward the men. This one hit and killed the man standing on the far side of the downed cow that was thrashing about on the ground and bawling weakly as her partially stripped hide flopped about her bloody body.

This time the remaining Mexican, now that he had seen where the shots had come from, returned Bannock's fire. A volley of shots were sent flying in his direction. Two of them kicked up dirt at the edge of the gully; two went whining over Bannock's head.

The two men who had been chasing the second cow wheeled their horses and were riding back to their companion. When they reached him, they leaped from their saddles and took cover behind the carcass of the partially skinned cow that merciful death had at last stilled.

Bannock ducked down low, his body pressed against the sloping side of the gulley for protection, as another volley of shots rang out. This one was louder and longer than the first one. So long, in fact, that Bannock was pinned down for several tense minutes. When the shooting finally subsided he risked a look over the rim of the gully. A shot whined over his head, forcing him back down into the gully again. He remained virtually motionless for several additional minutes during which more shots were fired at his position, all of which went harmlessly over his head.

When he risked another look at the three Mexicans some time later, he was surprised to find that they were all aboard their horses and heading away from him. A sense of quiet satisfaction swept through him. They were leaving. He had killed one of them and run the rest off. He stood up and reloaded his revolver. He was about to climb up out of the gully and head for his horse when he suddenly froze.

The Mexicans—all three of them—had turned toward him and were splitting up. One rode to the east, one to the west. The remaining man sat his saddle facing Bannock, who was well beyond the range of all of their guns.

He stood where he was, half in and half out of the gully, wondering what the three hide-peelers were up to. His eyes flicked between the two riders who were still heading east and west respectively. He watched them circle around and then begin riding toward each other. What they were doing made no sense to Bannock.

The two men turned. Then turned again. One of them shouted something in Spanish.

Bannock, watching, suddenly realized what they were doing. They were rounding up the cattle and beginning to drive them in his direction. The third man, who had not moved for some time, suddenly sprang to life again. He rode directly toward the cows their companions had driven in from the east and west. All three began to use the ropes that hung from their saddle horns to drive the bunched cows straight toward Bannock.

He considered making a run for it. But only briefly. Such a move would, he realized, be tantamount to suicide. The long line of cattle that was stampeding toward him—he could hear the clattering of some of the steers' horns as they struck other horns—would trample him to death if he ran either east or west before he could get beyond them. If he turned and ran in the same direction they were running it wouldn't be long before they overtook him.

Think, he told himself. There has to be a way out of this. I won't die like a dog trampled under the hooves of those cows.

But his mind was filled with noise that drowned out all thought. The brittle clattering of horns. The pounding of scores of hooves that were punishing the ground. The loudly shouted Spanish of the three Mexicans who were now all positioned behind the cattle they were so relentlessly driving straight toward Bannock.

Sweat broke out on his face and body as a cold fear seized him in its icy hands and shook him to his very soul.

FOUR

BANNOCK'S FEAR was replaced by a furious desire for action. He began to cough as the wind blew the dust of the stampeding cattle toward him. He dropped down on his knees to begin the execution of an idea that had occurred to him despite the draining fear he had been feeling. It was that idea that now fueled both his mind and body and kindled the hot fire of hope within him.

Holstering his gun, he began to dig into the soft dirt wall of the gully with his hands. He tore at the earth in his determination to rend it asunder. Dust and dirt flew in every direction as he scraped and clawed. Grunting with effort, his head bent and his jaw set, he hollowed out a hole that measured no more than four feet high and just over two feet wide.

As the first of the stampeding cattle leaped across the gully just above his head, Bannock rammed his body into the hole he had made. To make himself fit into it, he pulled his knees up to his chin and clasped them tightly in his arms. He turned his head and pressed his left cheek against the hollowed-out dirt wall.

He had no sooner done so than a steer crashed down into the gully. The animal lumbered to its feet and climbed up the far side of the gully and disappeared. Cows plowed and skidded down the side of the gully and then up the other side to race mindlessly on.

Bannock, feeling the heat of their bodies, continued to sweat. He hunkered under the ledge he had made above his head and prayed that his maneuver would save him from being crushed to death under the deadly hooves of the cattle. He shut his eyes as two steers fell down into the gully and then ran past him instead of trying to climb the bank on the opposite side. A long horn of one of the animals barely missed Bannock where he had taken refuge. When the steers had gone, he reached out and retrieved his gun.

Time passed. An eternity of time, it seemed. But at last his ordeal came to an end. No more cows leaped across or ran down into the gully. He could hear them stampeding away from the gully but gradually the sound began to fade.

It was replaced by words. Spanish words. Bannock knew enough Spanish to be able to understand most of the conversation that was taking place above him on the rim of the gully. The Mexicans were asking one another where he was. They were wondering what had happened to him. One of them suggested that he had been caught up in the herd and carried away with it. Someone else rejected that idea, ordering the two men with him to spread out along the bank of the gully and search for the "Anglo." When asked if he was coming, the man replied in the negative. He would, he said, stay right where he was until the other two men returned.

Bannock, not moving so much as a muscle, not even an eyelash, listened to the sound of boots crunching the earth as two of the Mexicans moved away, one heading east, the other west. He waited a minute. Two. Three. Then he picked up a small stone and tossed it across the gully. As it clattered down the slope into the bottom of the gully, he heard the lone man above him mutter, *"¿Que hay?"*

He drew his gun and continued to wait, hoping that curiosity might lure the cat above him down to where he could be taken.

Bannock's ploy worked. The Mexican gingerly slid down the side of the gully, gun in hand, his eyes roaming up and down the trough at the bottom of the cut.

Before his eyes could detect the man in his hollowed-out hiding place in the gully wall, Bannock barked, "Drop your gun!"

The Mexican turned swiftly in his direction. But before he could fire, Bannock shot the gun out of his hand. When the Mexican bent to retrieve it, Bannock fired again, hitting the gun and making it bounce along the dirt floor of the gully.

The Mexican straightened and raised his hands.

Bannock crawled out of the hole in the gully wall and stood up. He jerked a thumb, indicating to the Mexican that he was to climb up to level ground. The man obediently proceeded to do so, followed by Bannock, who had picked up the man's gun and thrust it into his waistband.

As he had expected, his captive's two companions were both riding back in response to the gunfire. When they spotted Bannock and his prisoner, they drew rein and their guns.

"You shoot and your friend here dies!" Bannock told them.

The men exchanged glances. They looked back at Bannock.

"Drop your guns!" he ordered them.

One did. One didn't.

When the one who hadn't dropped his gun fired a snap shot, Bannock drilled him in the right forearm. The gun fell from the wounded man's hand.

Bannock walked his prisoner over to the dropped guns and picked them up, one by one. He thrust them into his waistband to join the weapon he had taken from the man standing in front of him with his arms still up in the air.

"We're taking a little trip," he told all three men. "To town."

"Señor, we—"

"Shut up!" Bannock bellowed, rage rising red within him suddenly as he caught a glimpse of a bawling calf that was nuzzling the almost hideless body of the dead cow which was obviously its mother. "You," he said to his prisoner. "Climb up behind one of your friends."

"Señor, my horse—"

"Forget your horse, Do as I say and do it now!"

The man, with the help of one of the mounted Mexicans, climbed up behind the rider.

Bannock stepped into the saddle of his bay and gave a one-word order: "Move!"

The men moved their horses out.

As the Mexicans, with Bannock riding behind them with his gun drawn, rode into the town of Antelope they drew stares of curiosity and stares of hostility. Armed men and Mexicans were two breeds that the townsmen of Antelope had little or no use for.

Bannock ordered a halt in front of the marshal's office. He dismounted and ordered the Mexicans out of the saddle as well. When they had their feet on the ground and their hands in the air, he marched them into the office. The sandy-haired marshal, who had been sitting with his booted feet propped up on his desk, jumped to his feet; a single-sheet weekly edition of the *Antelope Herald* fluttered to the floor.

"What's this all about, Mr. Bannock?"

"Howdy, Marshal Metcalf. This is about hide-peeling. I caught these three—there were four but I had to shoot one of them—stripping the hide off one of Tom Butler's cows."

The marshal studied Bannock's prisoners. "What have you got to say for yourself?" he asked them.

The men remained mute as Metcalf's eyes came to rest on their bloodstained clothing.

"Inside," he ordered, jerking a thumb over his shoulder.

When he had his three prisoners secured in one of the cells behind his office, he returned, shaking his head. "I don't know what this old world of ours is coming to."

"If you ask me, I'd say it looks like it's heading for hell in a handbasket, what with hide-peeling and rustling Mexicans on the loose like they are."

"Every stockman within miles of here's having headaches with these greasers, seems like," Metcalf said as he sat back down behind his desk and waved Bannock into a chair.

"How many of these rustlers have you jailed?" Bannock asked bluntly as he sat down.

"Not many," Metcalf admitted somewhat sheepishly. "They're harder to catch than greased pigs."

"You've been out hunting them, have you?"

"Mr. Bannock, you're putting me on the hot spot. No, I haven't been out hunting them to tell you the gospel truth."

"Why not?"

"On account of I only had one deputy and he up and quit on me two weeks back. Antelope's not a rich town, as you no doubt know. They don't have much money to pay us law dogs."

"They might find paying for law dogging is a good investment if they find their town under attack as it well might be one of these days. From what I've heard—and experienced personally —that sad state of affairs just very well might come to pass before very long. Colonel Mantavo and his border bandits are getting bolder by the minute."

"Some folks, they're afraid of testifying against the greasers when their cases come to court. Fred Halston caught a pair of them trying to steal his horses. Caught them red-handed and turned them in to me. But when their trial came up, Fred was nowhere to be found. The case was dismissed for lack of evidence—made the circuit court judge madder than a wet hen. I went out to the Flats and asked Fred why he didn't put in an appearance and testify against those horse thieves. Fred told me he'd had himself a visit from some Mexicans who told him he didn't see nothing and he didn't know nothing about any horse thieves. They told him his health would suffer if he went to court. They would depend, they told Fred, on his good sense to keep his mouth shut. If he didn't, they said, he was as good as dead."

"I'll attend the trial of those three you've got locked up in there." Bannock assured Metcalf.

"The trial won't be for a while, you know. The circuit court judge was through here just last week. He won't be back for a month or more."

"Keep me posted, Marshal. I'll give evidence against those men when the time comes."

"I'll be sure to do that."

Bannock rose and left the office. An hour later, he was back on his own range and twenty minutes after that he was riding up to his ranch.

He dismounted and led his horse into the barn where he stripped his gear from it, rubbed the bay down and filled its feedbox with grain.

Once inside the house, he lit a lamp at his desk in a corner of the room and sat down to do the calculations with pencil and paper that he had been going over in his mind during his ride home.

Soon the paper was filled with numbers—how many feet of barbed wire it would take to fence in his ranch, the cost of the wire, the average per-head cost of each cow that he owned and the like. When he had finished some time later, he had come to the conclusion he had fully expected to reach. A conclusion validated by the facts and figures before him. It would cost him far less to fence his land, hire armed guards in addition to the men he already employed and fortify his holdings than it would to risk losing cattle to the marauding men under the command of Colonel Pedro Mantavo.

He turned down the lamp and went to bed. During the night he dreamed of Nora as he almost always did. He dreamed as well of faceless brush-riding bandits with guns in their hands and larceny in their black hearts.

After breakfast the following morning, he sent his cook for Wes Holbrook. When the foreman arrived at the house, Bannock told him about Tom Butler's decision to move his family north. "He's scared, Wes, and I don't blame him one bit for being so." He also told Holbrook about what Butler had told him had happened to Phil and Amelia McIntyre.

Holbrook whistled through his teeth. "I never heard tell of

such things before. Lord A'mighty, what's the world coming to?"

"There's more I've got to tell you," Bannock said glumly. "On the way home from Josh Cameron's funeral I ran into some hide-peelers. They were attacking Butler's stock, which, incidentally, I've agreed to buy from Tom." Bannock proceeded to tell Holbrook about the gunfight and the subsequent jailing of the three surviving hide-peelers in Antelope.

"Mantavo's men, do you reckon?"

"I do but I can't prove it and I suppose it doesn't matter. They're all the same sort of villains whether or not they happen to be taking orders from the Commander of the Line of the Bravo or not. By the way, I wrote out this draft for Tom." He handed it to his foreman and added, "I want you to ride down to Tom's place and give him that. Then you and some of the men can herd Tom's cattle—they're out on Gooseneck Flats—back here to our range."

Holbrook started to rise but Bannock waved him back into his chair. "There's another important matter I want to discuss with you. When I got home yesterday I did some figuring and I came up with the idea that we'd better fence in the ranch and fortify it too."

"Fence it? I always thought you were down on fences of any kind, Mr. Bannock."

"You're right, I was. I guess, in a way, I still am. But I've been thinking that fencing this place is the thing to do. You take a look down toward the border and you don't have to have eyes of an eagle to spot trouble riding this way. The only question, it seems to me, is when it's going to finally get here."

"It's your business what you do on your spread, Mr. Bannock," Holbrook said slowly, "but won't fence cost a pretty penny?"

"Indeed it will. But it'll cost more if those border ruffians make off with our stock—even a goodly portion of it. Like I said, I figured it out last night in dollars and cents and came to the conclusion that fence and fortifications will probably turn out to be well worth the money they'll cost. I consider them a prudent investment. In this connection, I've made up my mind to hire some new hands."

"We've got all we need right at the moment, Mr. Bannock."

"To do the work of normal times, yes, we do have enough for that. But I'm not sure we have enough to do the work of what are fast becoming *ab*normal times. The men I want to hire have to be handy with guns. Which reminds me. I want you and everybody else who works this place to go out armed from now on. Any man who doesn't have a gun and can't afford to buy himself one—tell him I'll buy one for him."

"How many more men do you want me to take on?"

"I'd say a half dozen ought to turn the trick. I'll leave it up to you to find them. But like I said, make sure they can at least hit the side of a barn they shoot at—and preferably a bull's-eye painted on the side of that barn."

Wes grinned. "I won't hire anybody who can't hit a fly at fifty paces, Mr. Bannock."

"Better make that a fly's eye, Wes." It was Bannock's turn to grin.

"What kind of fortifications for the ranch did you have in mind?"

"I want a tower built so that the guard manning it can spot trouble before it gets here. The fence will keep them at bay when they do get here and give us time to gather our forces and mount a counterattack."

"I'm not sure all the men are going to be happy about finding that they're hired on here to fight a war, Mr. Bannock."

"There will undoubtedly be some who won't want to stay on once they hear what you have to tell them. Pay off those who don't and let them ride out. I won't blame them if they want to leave. In fact, it's better to find out now and find out fast if there are any men around here who don't have the stomach for a fight in which they could get themselves killed. I don't want to find out that they don't want to fight once the trouble starts. That'll be too late and having them around then will only hurt us."

"I'll head down to Tom Butler's place," Wes said, rising, "and give him this." He held up Bannock's draft and then pocketed it. "I'll stop in Antelope on the way back and order the wire and lumber we'll need."

"I won't be here when you get back."

"You won't? Where—"

"I'm taking the train down to the border." Reading the question in Holbrook's eyes, Bannock said, "I'm going to pay a call on Major Endicott down at Fort Brown. Since we don't have any Texas Rangers around here anymore and lawmen like Marshal Metcalf in Antelope haven't got the manpower or will, in some cases, to put an end to the plunder and rapine that's taking place, I thought I might be able to get the Army to come to our aid."

"That's a fine and dandy idea, Mr. Bannock," Holbrook declared enthusiastically. "If we had army patrols roaming about between the Nueces valley and the Rio Bravo we wouldn't have a whole lot to worry about anymore. I wish you luck with the major."

"I'll see you when I get back, Wes. Meantime, you—"

"I'll see to it that our men are all armed and I'll hire some more gun-hung riders and start building the fence and the guard tower—don't you worry about me and the boys, Mr. Bannock. I reckon we're going to be about as busy as beavers in the days and weeks to come."

The sun was shining brightly when Bannock stepped down from the train the following afternoon at Brownsville. Bright enough and hot enough to remind him of the time he had spent recently in Yuma in Arizona Territory where the sun tended to blister a man the instant he stepped out into it.

He walked, carrying his carpet bag, to the Miller Hotel where he registered and was shown to a clean room on the second floor. Leaving his carpet bag unpacked—he didn't know how long he would be staying in the hotel—he left his room after washing up and went outside where he rented a carriage and drove to Fort Brown outside of town.

When he arrived, he asked a sentry patrolling the perimeter of the fort where he could find Major Endicott. He was directed to the fort's headquarters building where he found a corporal seated at a desk just inside the door.

"Sir?" said the soldier as Bannock took off his hat and wiped his face with an already damp handkerchief. "May I be of some help, sir?"

"I'd like to have a word with Major Endicott. My name's Bannock. Benjamin Bannock. I'm a cattleman from the Nueces River Valley."

"May I tell the major the nature of your business with him, sir?"

"I'm here to talk to him about another soldier—one from south of the border named Colonel Pedro Mantavo."

The corporal left the room. When he returned a few minutes later, it was to usher Bannock into an austerely furnished office at the rear of the building. A middle-aged man seated behind a rickety desk looked up as he entered and then rose and held out his hand.

"I'm Major Charles Endicott," he announced, shaking hands with his visitor. "And you're Mr. Benjamin Bannock come to talk about the depredations being wreaked on the citizens of this fair state of Texas by one Colonel Pedro Mantavo. Sit you down and I'll listen to what you have to say."

The goateed and mustachioed major sat down and Bannock did the same.

"You're familiar with the activities of the Mantavo band, I take it," Bannock remarked, meeting Major Endicott's steady green-eyed gaze.

"I am. He has been raiding farther and farther into Texas territory of late."

"To begin at the beginning and to put things bluntly, Major, I've come here today to ask your help in stopping Mantavo and his raiders on behalf of myself and other Texas stockmen like myself whose lives and property Colonel Mantavo has placed in jeopardy."

"Let me hasten to say, sir, that you have my deepest and sincerest sympathy. Your plight is a lamentable one—yours and those who share it. But I am afraid there is really very little, if anything at all, that I can do for you."

"You have men under your command who could patrol the area, do you not?" Bannock asked, his ire rising at the blandness of his reception by the major.

"Infantry, Mr. Bannock, infantry. Let me remind you that Texas is a vast state. Infantry cannot properly patrol it. Even if they had legitimate orders to attempt to do so."

Endicott's last remark suggested to Bannock the way this conversation was going to go and it also suggested how it was going to end. But he nevertheless persevered.

"Cavalry could—"

"There are no cavalry troops stationed here at Fort Brown. There are some troops of the Eighth Cavalry stationed to the north at Ringgold Barracks but not enough, however, to accomplish the task you have in mind. Why, the border alone is hundreds of miles long and would require all their resources—and a great deal more—to adequately patrol it. As for the interior—" Endicott shrugged and held out his hands, palms up, in a gesture signifying helplessness.

"Surely one of the duties of you and your men, Major, is to protect the lives and property of the people in this region is it not?"

"Our orders are to keep the peace, insofar as possible, along the border."

"Well, there you are, Major. Doesn't that imply the protection of the people in your jurisdiction?"

"Mr. Bannock, do you know that most of the people living north of the border for a matter of many miles are, in the main, Mexican nationals? They outnumber Anglos, outside of the towns that is, by something like one hundred to one.

"Please, sir," Endicott continued, holding up a hand to silence the protest Bannock had been about to make. "The duty you speak of involving me and my infantrymen is not to protect Mexicans. To do so would be not without its irony, I submit to you."

"I don't understand, Major."

"You may not realize it, Mr. Bannock, but many if not most of the Mexicans of whom I speak are well aware of the activities of Colonel Mantavo. Many of these people actively aid and abet the colonel in both small and large ways. To protect them—if such a thing were required under my military mandate, which it decidedly is not—would be to protect, in effect, Colonel Mantavo himself."

"Are you telling me that there is nothing you can do to protect the people of Texas who are suffering at the hands of this brigand, Major?"

Another shrug. "If my superiors should change my orders I will obey them but, as I've tried to explain to you, Mr. Bannock, at the present time I am not under orders to send my men anywhere but along the border."

"They are apparently not doing a very good job of patrolling the border," Bannock responded heatedly. "Mexican rustlers and horse thieves cross at will in either direction and move American stock into Mexico as easily as fleas ride a blue tick hound."

"What do you expect us to do? Apprehend every man, woman and child who crosses the border? Some of them live here, for God's sake. *Here.* In Texas. They go south on occasion to visit relatives. They come back."

"Do they go south with herds of cattle in tow, Major?"

"We are soldiers, Mr. Bannock, not stock inspectors. We do not know one brand from another. We do not know who owns the cattle that cross the border. It is your job and the job of civilians like you who have a vested interest in this matter to deal with the problem."

"We have tried, Major. In the past, our Stockmen's Association has sent inspectors to examine every cow and every hide

66　　　　　　　　　L E O　P.　K E L L E Y

that leaves Texas and crosses the Rio Bravo into Mexico. Two of
those inspectors have been killed. Murdered by person or persons unknown. Person or persons no doubt connected to Colonel Mantavo."

"May I make a suggestion, Mr. Bannock?"

When Bannock nodded, Major Endicott said, "Why not peti-
tion your representatives and senators in Washington? The cattlemen have power. You have influence by virtue of your contri-
bution to the economy of the state and the nation itself. Ask for
help. Ask that the United States Government intervene in this
ugly situation with Mexico. Maybe such action would put a stop
to the problem once and for all. It seems to me to be worth a try
at least."

"Our Stockmen's Association has done just that. We have
received letters, telegraph messages—they all say the same
thing. Our problem is a local one. The government does not
want to get involved with it because it might strain relations with
the sovereign state of Mexico. Hogwash is what it all amounts
to."

Major Endicott lit a cigar, a long nine. He blew smoke into the
room in perfect circles, careful to keep it away from Bannock,
who was sitting tensely on the edge of his chair.

"I'm sorry to have taken up your time," Bannock said, rising.

"One moment, sir."

Bannock waited.

"You've come all the way down here to talk to me."

"To no avail."

"Through no fault, really, of my own."

Grudgingly: "Granted."

"Before you turn around and head home, why not pay a call
on the mayor of Matamoros?"

Bannock raised an eyebrow.

"Why not? What have you got to lose? Maybe a personal visit
from a cattleman such as yourself who represents powerful in-
terests in the United States would have some effect upon him. It
might even persuade him to crack down on Colonel Mantavo's

traffic in stolen stock. You are a persuasive man, Mr. Bannock—"

"I haven't been able to persuade you to take action against the thieves."

"That is simply because I am but a cog in a great military machine that clangs and clanks along and sometimes—*sometimes,* I say—can get things done and done properly. At other times—" Another of the major's characteristic shrugs. "Talk to the mayor. His name is Xavier Coronel. I have met him and he is a most charming gentleman. If you can't persuade him to get Mantavo to pull in his horns, perhaps you could threaten him."

"Threaten him? With what?"

"Use your imagination. You referred a moment ago to your Stockmen's Association, did you not?"

"Yes, but I don't see—"

"You might tell the *alcalde* that you and the members of your organization are contemplating making a raid on Colonel Mantavo's rancho near Matamoros. You could tell him that you're fully aware of the fact that such an action would without a doubt create an international incident which might prove most embarrassing to Señor Coronel as a dully constituted civil authority since you had first turned to him for aid but your pleas, unfortunately, fell on deaf ears.

"Let me tell you, if you do not already know, that Señor Coronel, as *alcalde* of Matamoros, possesses not only administrative powers in his official position as mayor but also—and this is important, Mr. Bannock—judicial powers as well. Ask Señor Coronel to use those judicial powers that he has at his disposal against Colonel Mantavo so that you will not be forced to take certain actions on your own. Actions which could make matters difficult for him with his own government.

"Such a ploy might not work. But, then again, it just might. And Matamoros is just across the river from Brownsville. It might prove to have been worth the time and trouble for you to pay a call on the *alcalde* of Matamoros, Mr. Bannock."

"I think I begin to understand now how you have reached the rank that you have, Major."

"What do you mean?"

"You excel as a strategist. I'm sure that is an asset to any military man."

"Mr. Bannock, I grew up in the hills of Tennessee. When I was a boy I learned many things—how to hunt, how to fish, how to forecast the weather and so on. I also learned that there is more than one way to skin a skunk. But please don't quote me when you call on Señor Coronel."

"I won't breathe a word, Major."

Endicott rose and shook hands with Bannock. "I'm sorry I could not be of more help to you, sir."

"If I should decide to launch a raid into Mexico at some point in the future—me and a few other hotheaded Texas cattlemen—maybe you and your men will come to our rescue if we get ourselves into serious trouble."

"It would be my pleasure, Mr. Bannock, I assure you."

Bannock left the office and returned to his carriage. He climbed into the carriage and drove back to Brownsville.

During the return trip, he went over in his mind what options he had available to him. There weren't that many. He briefly considered paying a visit to Ringgold Barracks where Endicott had said there were some cavalry troopers stationed. Could they be persuaded to patrol the area between the Rio Bravo on the south and the Nueces on the north?

No, he decided, I would be likely to get the same story from the commanding officer at Ringgold Barracks that I got from Endicott. No orders for such patrols. Not enough men even if there were such orders. Texas was a vast place, he could hear the officer in charge telling him. An impossible task. Why didn't he consider enlisting the aid of local authorities? Civilian authorities?

He thought about Endicott's suggestion.

Could he actually organize a raid into Mexico to recover whatever stolen cattle he and his riders could find and, in the process, put the fear of, not God, but Texas cattlemen into the larcenous hearts of Colonel Mantavo and his brush-riding bandits?

He doubted that such a plan would work. Even if he could get enough men to agree to ride with him on such an illegal excursion he suspected it would be him and them who would wind up in trouble for violating the sovereignity of Old Mexico. Major Endicott and his infantrymen might well be ordered to track down and imprison him and his raiders.

Endicott did, however, have a point in suggesting such a course of action. Or, rather, the threat of such action made in person to Xavier Coronel, the *alcalde* of Matamoros. Sure, it was a bluff and, sure, maybe Coronel would recognize it as such. On the other hand . . .

It was that other hand that intrigued Bannock and brought the ghost of a smile to his face. He decided then and there, as the carriage lurched and bounced over the rough trail that led back to Brownsville, what he would do. He would go to Matamoros. In the morning. First thing. Coronel, he thought, watch out. Here I come.

It was dusk when he pulled up in front of the livery, returned his rented rig and then headed for the saloon across the street. He went through the batwings and made his way across the sawdust-strewn floor and up to the bar.

"Whiskey," he told the bar dog. When a bottle and glass had been placed in front of him, he poured himself a drink and promptly downed it. Then, turning, he braced his elbows on the bar behind him and watched the one woman in the room as she moved from table to table and man to man, talking, laughing, chucking a drinker here, a gambler there, under their chins.

He had seen her the moment he had entered the bar and she, he knew for certain, had also seen him. Their eyes had met, held for a second, then drifted away. Now she seemed to be totally oblivious to his presence. But was she really?

His eyes roamed up and down her lush figure, noting her long lean legs in black lisle stockings, her pinched-in waist below her

provocative breasts and revealing cleavage. Her face was un-
marred—smooth as cream and faintly rosy. Her eyes were al-
mond and her hair, the color of ripe corn, was piled high on her
head in a tight nest of ringlets. He estimated her age at no more
than twenty. Twenty-two tops.

He willed her to look at him. She didn't. He made his way over
to the faro table in a corner of the room, making it a point to
pass by her.

She looked up at him as he paused by her side. He touched
the brim of his hat to her and then moved on. Did she smile? An
image of her pinked lips lingered in his mind as he reached the
faro table and placed four bits on the ten of diamonds.

"All set, gents?" asked the dealer standing behind the table.
Two other latecomers placed their bets—one on the tray of
clubs, the other on the ace of spades.

The dealer swept his gaze around the table and then, when no
more bets were placed, he said, "Who'll get lucky this turn,
gents?" and slid a card out of the slot in the wooden box that sat
on top of the table.

A gambler groaned as the dealer said, "First card in each turn
is the dealer's card. You lose, sir." He collected the gold eagle
that the gambler who had groaned had placed on the jack of
hearts, the card the dealer had just drawn.

A second card was drawn to complete the turn.

The five of clubs.

Bannock's eyes flicked to the dealer's helper, who was main-
taining the "case-keeper," an abacus-like device which told at a
glance how many cards of each suit had been played at any given
moment.

Five remained in the suit of diamonds. Bannock let his bet
ride.

The dealer drew the first card in the next turn and two men
lost their bets. The second, or winning, card brought a cheer
from the throat of the lone man who had bet on it. The dealer
paid off.

Minutes later, the case-keeper indicated that three cards in the suit of diamonds remained to be played. Bannock continued to let his original bet ride.

On the next turn, he won and the dealer paid. He glanced at the case-keeper and saw that two clubs remained to be played. Since he had joined the game, he had seen one club played. He had no way of knowing which other clubs had been played before his arrival. With only the briefest of hesitations, he placed his eight bits—his original four and his winnings—on the nine of clubs.

The first card in the third turn was the six of hearts.

The second was the king of spades. No clubs appeared on the next turn either. Bannock continued to let his bet ride.

The nine of clubs was the first card to appear in the next turn. Bannock watched the dealer rake in the eight bits he had bet.

"You don't look like a loser."

"I thank you kindly for the compliment," Bannock told the woman he had had his eye on who had just spoken to him and was now standing beside him at the faro table.

"I haven't seen you in here before, have I?"

"Nope, you've not."

"I would have remembered."

Their eyes met. Held.

"Can I buy you a drink?"

"You can buy it but it would be throwing money away."

"You look to me like a woman worth throwing money away for."

"I thank you for the compliment. But what I meant was the drinks they serve us—hostesses—are really only tea or water, depending on whether we order whiskey or gin."

"I see."

"But I could use a drink. To celebrate."

"It's your birthday."

"No. I meant to celebrate meeting you."

"You want tea or water?"

The woman shook her head. "I have a bottle of French brandy

in my room upstairs. It came all the way from New Orleans. Do you like brandy—French brandy?"

"I'm partial to anything French."

The woman's lips parted. She licked them. "Really?"

"Really."

She took his arm and they made their way over to the stairs on one side of the bar which led to the second floor.

"You can call me Marie," the woman said as they began to climb the stairs. "That's a French name."

"I know." Bannock strongly suspected that his companion's name wasn't really Marie. That name, he suspected, had been made up on the spur of the moment to suit their earlier bantering exchange. Her name was probably Molly or Ida or something equally mundane. He didn't care. He cared only about what awaited him once they were inside her room on the second floor.

FIVE

THE FOLLOWING MORNING, after sleeping later than he had planned to and eating a hearty breakfast in the hotel's dining room, Bannock made his way to the town's livery stable where he rented himself a roan for the journey to Matamoros.

After crossing the Rio Bravo south of town, he found himself in a noisy city of white adobe buildings that sparkled in the sun, almost blinding him. The streets were filled with people. Men on donkeys, women bearing produce in baskets or clay jars full of water drawn from the well in the plaza, children chasing a dog which had tin cans tied to its tail.

Wagons, horses pulling two-wheeled *carretas* and people pushing goods of all kinds piled high in wheelbarrows passed Bannock on both sides as he rode down the middle of the street. Vendors called out to the passing parade of people from their stands along the sides of the road, urging the purchase of their wares—chilis, tomatoes, pumpkins, pinto beans and the like.

A baby wrapped in the folds of a serape howled for no apparent reason. The dog with the tin cans clattering behind it began to bark and snap at the offending attachments to the delight of the chasing children.

The din was almost deafening but it didn't seem to bother the natives of the town. They smiled and laughed among themselves, their white teeth flashing in their dusky faces.

Bannock rode past an impressive church with a tall bell tower. When a tonsured priest wearing a brown robe and sandals emerged from the building's dim interior, he stopped and asked directions to the ranch of the *alcalde*. The priest pointed and told him in heavily accented English where the mayor's residence was located.

Bannock thanked the man and rode on, rounding the church and riding in the building's shadow down a wide street that eventually led him to his destination.

The rancho of the *alcalde* stood by itself at the end of the street. It was a square, solidly built, two-story building with a wraparound veranda on the second floor. It towered above its outbuildings, which were squat one-story structures. From behind the house came the sound of laughter—both men's and women's—and music.

Bannock, as he dismounted in front of the house and wrapped his reins around the hitch rail fronting it, heard the sounds of a guitar, violin and flute. The notes blended gaily with the laughter drifting on the breeze. He rounded the house and found himself on the edge of a huge throng of people dancing in the open space behind the dwelling.

The women wore festive gowns and shawls; the men were dressed in finery worthy of princes of the realm as they all danced the *contradanza*.

Bannock stood watching and listening to the music as the dancers dipped and swayed, came together and separated. Before he knew what he was doing, he was tapping the toe of his right boot on the ground in time with the music.

A fat man, with a red sash wrapped tightly about his ample girth, danced with a much younger woman. The man, noticing him, smiled in welcome, whispered something in the woman's ear and left her. As he approached Bannock, he held out his hand.

"Señor, you are welcome," he declared expansively, shaking Bannock's hand. "I am Xavier Coronel and this is my home. May I ask your name?"

"It's Ben Bannock. I'm sorry to bust in on you like this, *alcalde,* but I—"

"It is a pleasure to have you here. We celebrate—have been celebrating for two days, I should say—my daughter's wedding to Miguel Almonte. That is my jewel with whom I was just dancing."

Bannock studied the woman the mayor pointed out. She was a lithe and thoroughly lovely young woman with hair and eyes of ebony and a silken skin the color of pecans. She wore an elaborate headdress that was as white as her gown. White satin slippers adorned her dainty feet. She stood talking to a square-jawed young man whose eyes grew dreamy every time he looked at her.

"My new son-in-law," said the *alcalde,* nodding toward the young man. "I should hate him for taking from me the light of my life but I do not. He is a good man, is Miguel. He will take care of my Magdalena and give her many beautiful children."

"Señor Coronel, I came here to have a talk with you about a matter of the utmost importance. Would it be possible for us to speak in private?"

"Now? Here?"

"I realize I've arrived at a bad time but I've come a long way—all the way from just south of the Nueces River in Texas—"

"What is it you wanted to talk to me about, Mr. Bannock? What business does a man from north of the border have with the *alcalde* of Matamoros?"

Bannock never got to answer Coronel's question because at that moment Miguel Almonte, the bridegroom, hurried up to his father-in-law and said, "It is time to play the game with the rooster. Will you join us?"

"Ah, no, not this time," Coronel replied, shaking his head. Turning to Bannock, he explained, "My son-in-law speaks of a game we often play at such festivities. We bury a live rooster up to its neck in the ground and then ride down upon it and try to pull it free. It is a game for young and daring men and I am too

old and cautious now for such risky pastimes. Perhaps you
would like to play, Mr. Bannock?"

Almonte glanced at Bannock. "Have we met, señor?"

"No, we haven't," Bannock answered. He introduced himself
to Almonte.

"You are welcome to our celebration, señor," Almonte told
him. "And to the game we are about to play should you wish to
join it."

"I'll watch."

Almonte smiled. "As you wish. Rooster pulling is a dangerous
game as my father-in-law suggested. Especially if one is not a
skilled horseman."

Bannock said nothing as the smiling Almonte left to join
several other men who were saddling some horses.

"Watch," Coronel said, clasping his hands contentedly across
his bulging stomach.

Bannock, watching as a man buried a rooster in the ground
with only its head and neck showing, said, "About our talk,
Señor Coronel—"

"Not now, if you please," the man said, waving a hand in
dismissal of Bannock's words. "The game it begins."

Bannock watched as the men with Almonte all climbed
aboard their horses as did the bridegroom himself. The first
man to move out came galloping down a wide expanse of hard-
packed earth toward the rooster helplessly imprisoned in the
ground. As the man neared his goal, he bent down low on one
side of his saddle. Gripping his reins with his left hand, he let his
right hand dangle. Then, as he reached the rooster, he made a
fast grab for it.

Bannock could have sworn the rooster ducked. At any rate,
the man missed his target and went galloping on, his face a grim
mask of frustration.

A second man headed for the rooster, his horse's hooves
slamming against the ground. He overshot his goal. His grab for
the rooster had come just seconds too late. He rode on, giving
way to Miguel Almonte. The bridegroom made a dash for the

rooster, slashing his horse with his reins as he rode at a full gallop.

He slid so far down the side of his horse that Bannock was sure the man was going to fall. But he didn't. He kept his wide-open black eyes on the rooster and, at precisely the right instant, he reached out with his right hand and firmly seized the bird by the neck. It squawked in fear as its buried body was torn free of the earth. Holding his trophy high above his head and smiling broadly, he wheeled his horse and rode back to where his father-in-law and Bannock stood watching him, the elder man applauding wildly and the wedding guests cheering and whistling their approval of Almonte's deft performance.

"Lucky," he said self-deprecatingly as he drew rein and handed the rooster to a servant who had come running up to him.

He dismounted and watched the servant once again bury the squawking rooster in the ground to give the remaining game-players their chance at the prize.

"Not good luck," Bannock commented. "Good horsemanship."

Almonte glanced at him. Gave him a pleased grin.

"Excuse me, gentlemen. I'm going to get my horse."

"You have changed your mind?" Almonte asked him. "You will join our game then?"

"Not exactly. Or, I should say, I plan to play a variation of your game that I've had a go at once or twice in my time." Bannock dug down into his pocket and came up with a gold eagle, which he held up between two fingers.

Almonte and Coronel exchanged puzzled glances.

Bannock left them and stood apart, waiting until the rooster, like some exotic plant that had put in a miraculous appearance among the more mundane daisies and Jack-in-the-pulpits, was once again uprooted by a wildly whooping rider.

As the cheers began to die down, Bannock walked out to a spot near where the rooster had been. He bent down and placed the gold eagle flat on the ground. Then he went and got his roan, which he led to the makeshift starting line the game's contestants had been using. He swung into the saddle, settled himself and then spurred his horse into action.

His mount went galloping across the hardpan. Bannock never once took his gaze from the gold coin lying on the ground and glinting in the light of the sun. Nor did he for an instant let his attention waver from the difficult task he had set for himself.

Dust rose around him as he rode but he refused to let it bother or blind him. The gold eagle seemed to beckon to him. He let go of his reins and began to slip slowly down the side of his horse. His left hand tightly gripped his saddle horn. His right leg was doubled up and bent at a sharp angle, his right foot still firmly braced in its stirrup. His left foot had left its stirrup and was now neatly hooked behind the cantle of his saddle.

He reached out . . .

The coin seemed to come flying toward him . . .

With one swift move, he had it in his fingers and then clutched tightly in his fisted right hand.

The crowd was silent as he rode on, slowly bringing his horse to a walk.

Then, shaking off their surprise and silent awe of what Bannock had just done—the nearly impossible—they began to cheer and loudly applaud him. As he turned his bay and rode back toward them, a series of *"Oles"* rose from the crowd.

Miguel Almonte came running toward him. The bridegroom was vigorously shaking Bannock's hand and running along beside him as he did so.

Then, when Bannock brought his horse to a halt, the breathless Almonte exclaimed, *"Madre de Dios!* I have never in my life seen done a thing like what you just did, Señor Bannock. *Muy bueno!"*

Xavier Coronel came bustling and puffing up to them. "A miracle I have seen, Señor Bannock. Truly. You are *el impudente* indeed."

"Not so bold really," Bannock said modestly. "I used to practice doing what I just did. It gets easier over time."

"A toast!" Coronel cried to his guests. He beckoned and a servant bearing a silver tray on which rested gold goblets containing a dark red wine came hurrying up to him. Coronel took two goblets from the tray. He handed one to Bannock and one to his son-in-law. Then he took one for himself and sent the servant moving among the guests.

When everyone was ready, he raised his goblet. "To our visitor from *el norte*—a brave and bold man. May his days be filled with peace and plenty and his heart with all it deserves and desires."

Flowery speech, Bannock thought, as the people raised their goblets in his honor and then drank from them. That toast he just made could backfire on a man. That part about a heart being filled with all it deserves and desires. That wish, if granted, just might kill a man, depending upon what his heart happens to deserve and desire. But the old man meant well and I'm not one to quibble. He drained his goblet.

"Now we shall feast—again," Coronel declared, rubbing his belly, rolling his eyes and licking his lips. To Bannock, he said in an aside, "We have done nothing but feast for two days. It is a good thing I do not have another daughter to marry off anytime soon. I would, if I did, soon become a veritable mountain of a man." He laughed heartily and, beckoning to Bannock, made his way over to where a long table draped in white linen stood in the cool shade of a mesquite tree. Food covered almost every inch of it, Bannock discovered. There were bowls and platters filled with enchiladas, tortillas, a rice soup, and other things he did not recognize.

"Try this," Coronel suggested, pointing to a steaming bowl filled with meat and fruit. "We call it *puchero.* It is a tasty stew. And this—have some *nixtamal.* It is a corn porridge. You can wash it all down with some *champurrado*—in English—hot chocolate."

"I appreciate your hospitality, Señor Coronel, but I really would rather sit down in private with you and discuss the matter that has brought me here today."

"Yes, yes, we will do that. In a moment, *sí.*" Coronel heaped a plate high with food and then, turning to Bannock, he asked, "You will have nothing?"

"I'm not hungry."

Coronel popped a black olive into his mouth and, chewing and juggling his plate and a cup he had filled with *champurrado,* beckoned.

Bannock followed him as he made his way toward the back door of his home. The two men entered the hot kitchen and then went down a long hall. Coronel turned right into a study that was richly furnished with heavy furniture and ceiling-high shelves lined with leather-bound books. He sat down behind a sturdy desk and indicated that his guest was also to seat himself.

Bannock did. "I've come about the cattle rustling that's been going on in southern Texas, Señor Coronel. It is rapidly reaching a point that is totally intolerable."

"Rustling, *sí.* It is a scourge, is it not? When I was a young man"—Coronel forked food into his mouth, chewed—"I worked on a rancho not far from Mexico City. All of us *vaqueros* were constantly having to fight off rustlers. They stole our cows and would have stolen our hats had we not kept our hands on them."

He laughed lightly and ate another black olive.

"I'm sorry to say the rustlers in this instance are some of your own people."

Coronel didn't even look up from his plate as he continued to stuff himself. "Mexicans, you say? That is no surprise. As I just said, when I was a young man rustlers—*Mexican* rustlers—"

Bannock interrupted. "The word is they are being led—or at least supervised—by Colonel Pedro Mantavo."

Coronel looked up from his plate, his eyes narrowing. "You have proof of this?"

"No. But I've been told that Mantavo is responsible. I came here in the hope of enlisting your aid in your official capacity as *alcalde* of Matamoros in putting a stop to the practice by putting a stop to Mantavo."

"But you tell me you have no proof that Colonel Mantavo is involved in this rustling you speak of. How then, Mr. Bannock, am I to assist you in the matter when you can only accuse but not prove your accusations?"

The conversation he had had with Major Endicott echoed in Bannock's mind. "Maybe you could do a little investigating on this side of the border while I and other stockmen do a little of our own up north."

"But, my dear Mr. Bannock, what is there to investigate?"

"I've just told you. Investigate the comings and the goings and the doings of Colonel Pedro Mantavo and the men associated with him."

"Colonel Mantavo is a much respected man in Mexico, Mr. Bannock. He distinguished himself during the war. He is a national hero. I would not dare to investigate such a man."

"Maybe there are other ways of handling this then. Maybe I ought to round up some of the stockmen in Texas who've seen some of the rustlers—as I have—and then the whole bunch of us can ride down here and deliver some American justice since we can't seem to get any of the Mexican kind."

"Mr. Bannock—"

Coronel was interrupted by a knock on the door of his office. He got up and flung open the door. "I am busy now—"

As Bannock glanced over the mayor's shoulder he saw a hand reach out and deposit a bulky envelope in Coronel's hand. He heard a brief exchange in Spanish but the words were hastily whispered so he could not make them out.

Coronel returned to his desk but he did not sit down. Stuffing the envelope he had been handed into the pocket of his coat, he said, "I must go now, Mr. Bannock. I have just been informed of the arrival of an important guest and I, as host of the celebration taking place here today, must go and greet him personally. You, Mr. Bannock, may want to come with me since the guest of whom I speak is none other than Colonel Pedro Mantavo."

"He's here?" Bannock shot to his feet.

Coronel nodded. "I hope you will do nothing to embarrass him in front of my other guests."

"I don't want to cause you or your guests any trouble. But I do think I ought to get Mantavo off into a corner somewhere and have a heart-to-heart talk with him."

Bannock followed Coronel out of the office as the man hurried to greet his newly arrived guest. Outside, pandemonium reigned supreme, he discovered. Coronel's guests were clustered around a tall man, everyone talking at once and loudly.

As Coronel scuttled over to his newly arrived guest, Bannock noted the imperious look in the man's eyes. Although he was smiling broadly and even bowing to those gathered around him, his smile never reached his eyes and his bows were condescending, not the least bit humble. He wore the impressive uniform of the Mexican Army and it added to the unmistakable aura of authority he projected.

His eyes were amber, not the black of most Mexicans, and his hair, though black, had a faint touch of gold in it here and there, which might have had something to do with the way the sun struck it. His nose was a bit too large for his face but his solidly square chin took away some of the dominance of that particular feature. His cheekbones were prominent and hinted of Indian blood flowing in his veins. Altogether, a fine figure of a man, Bannock had to admit, however grudgingly, to himself.

"*Alcalde,*" Colonel Mantavo said, after holding up a slender but strong hand for silence, which the crowd instantly granted him. "I have brought a small gift for your daughter, Magdalena." He handed the young bride a small white box.

Miguel Almonte moved closer to her and put an arm around his wife. The crowd was silent as Magdalena lifted the lid of the box. A cry of delight escaped her lips. Smiling, she turned in a circle to display the contents of the box to those gathered around her.

Ooohhs and *aaahhs* greeted the revelation of the ruby earrings the box contained.

Magdalena held one of them up so all could be sure to see.

"Gracias, señor," she said shyly to the colonel as the sun pierced the blood-red jewel in her hand and made it sparkle.

"You are too kind, Colonel," Coronel breathed, staring transfixed at the ruby earring in his daughter's upraised hand. "I thank you from the bottom of my heart for remembering my Magdalena on this, one of the happiest days of her life."

"De nada," Mantavo responded expansively. "I wish you and your new husband well in all the days to come, Magdalena. I wish you both much happiness and hope that you and your father and your husband will remain good friends of the house of Mantavo."

"That is our promise to you, sir," Miguel Almonte responded firmly and sincerely.

"It is a privilege the house of Mantavo grants us," Coronel added. Then, "Come, Colonel. There is much to eat and drink. And soon there will be dancing."

"Forgive me, *alcalde,"* Mantavo said. "But I am pressed for time. I would very much like to stay and join in your celebration but I have things I must do. You will forgive—and excuse—me?"

"Certainly," Coronel responded quickly, although Bannock saw the disappointment in the man's eyes. "Of course. A man of your stature—of your important station in life—there are many things—many people—who make demands on you, I know. Let me just say again that you have the heartfelt thanks of me and mine for having taken time from your busy day to come here and grace us all with your presence."

Mantavo headed for the front of the house where a carriage and driver awaited him.

Bannock hurried after him. When he caught up with him on the side of the house, he said, "Colonel Mantavo, my name's Ben Bannock and I'd like to have a word with you."

Mantavo studied Bannock without speaking for a moment. Then, smiling, he said, "You are a guest of the Coronels? I don't believe we have met before. You are not from this area, that is so?"

"I'm from Texas. I came to see the *alcalde* to ask him what he intended to do about the cattle rustling that's been taking place north of the border. Now I've come to talk to you about the same thing."

"I am frankly bewildered, Mr. Bannock. What has cattle rustling in Texas to do with me or the mayor of Matamoros?"

"I think you know the answer to that question, Colonel."

"On the contrary—"

"You're behind it," Bannock stated bluntly.

"How dare you, Mr. Bannock!" Mantavo exclaimed. "You do not know me and yet you make an outrageous accusation against me. You are insulting, sir, and I am tempted to seek satisfaction."

"I do know you, Mantavo. Everybody south of the Nueces River up in Texas knows you—or about you. They've either had cattle stolen from them by you or they know about somebody who has."

Coronel came running up to them in time to hear Bannock's last words.

"My dear Colonel Mantavo," he spluttered, his wet lips working, "I offer you a thousand apologies. This man came here today out of nowhere. He said many bad things about you, Colonel, all of which I am sure are untrue. I have asked him— pleaded with him—not to disrupt this happy day but he is, as you can see, a determined man and a bit of a boor. Now I shall ask him to leave. Mr. Bannock—"

"One moment," a calm Mantavo said, holding up a restraining hand. "The man amuses me in a way. Tell me, Mr. Bannock, how do you intend to prove the accusation you have so glibly made against me just now?"

"I haven't got any proof—"

"Aha!" crowed Mantavo.

"Talk," said Coronel dismissively. "All talk. Words without meaning." He pulled a white linen handkerchief from his pocket and swabbed his sweating brow. "I should have sent this troublemaker away when your driver came to my door and told me you were here. Now—"

"I'll get proof, Mantavo," Bannock declared, his eyes never leaving the colonel's. "Even if I don't get any, I'm hell-bent on stopping you and the bandits who ride for you."

"You dare to threaten me," Mantavo muttered, his eyes afire. "You accuse me and then admit you cannot prove the accusation you make against me. Then you dare to stand there and threaten me. I will not have it. No man can treat me like that. No man will. That includes you, Bannock."

"Is that a threat, Colonel?"

"It is. One I will, should you attempt to make trouble for me, make good on."

Mantavo turned on his heels and strode toward his carriage. Bannock went after him, intending to try again to get him to admit that he and men he employed had indeed been rustling Texas cattle. But when Bannock reached him, he stopped in his tracks and could only stare at the man seated in the carriage.

He had seen—and met—the man before and he immediately recalled their nearly deadly meeting. Mantavo's driver was one of the two armed Mexicans who had attempted to rustle Tom Butler's cattle. The one who had almost blown Bannock's ear off during the subsequent gunfight.

"That man," Bannock said, pointing to the carriage driver. "He's my proof."

Mantavo glanced over his shoulder. "You are talking about my driver, Diego Anza?"

"I am. I ran into him the other day, him and another Mexican. They were trying to steal some cattle belonging to a friend of mine. I helped run them off. But not before he or the man with him killed a man who worked for my friend."

"Surely you are mistaken," Mantavo said. "Diego has not been out of Mexico in a very long time. He could not have done what you say he did. Mr. Bannock, I think you are mistaken—I *know* you are mistaken."

"There's no mistake," Bannock insisted. "That's the man that nearly shot my ear off, dammit!"

"I will not tolerate this. The mere fact that you claim you saw Diego—that you claim you saw him north of the border—that is proof of nothing. So what then do we have? A contretemps is what we have. We have your word against his."

"No, we have something much more than that. We have his word and *my* word as well against yours, Mr. Bannock. If you were to try to press your charges with the mayor here, I'm sure they would, in the bitter end, come to nothing."

Coronel nodded briskly, his eyes darting back and forth between the two men.

"You know something," Bannock said. "I think you're right, Colonel. I think the *alcalde* here is one of your boys, that's what I think."

Coronel began to splutter with indignation but Bannock silenced him as he continued, "The *alcalde* said a moment ago, as I recollect the conversation, that this Diego Anza of yours was the man who came to his office to announce your arrival. Have I got this right?"

"I sent him to summon Señor Coronel, *sí.*"

"I saw Anza hand an envelope to the *alcalde.* I saw the *alcalde* stuff it into the pocket of his coat. What was in that envelope, Colonel? Señor Coronel?"

Both men glared at Bannock. Neither man answered his question.

"Let's find out," Bannock said. He reached out and, before Coronel could stop him, he had ripped the envelope from the man's coat pocket, opened it and displayed the Mexican folding money it contained.

"That money—" Mantavo began and hesitated. "That money was in payment for some—goods I purchased from the mayor."

"Yes, for goods," Coronel echoed.

Bannock's expression was one of utter disbelief. "What goods exactly?"

"Grain," Mantavo said as Coronel said, "Horses."

The *alcalde* wilted under the colonel's indicting stare. "I made a mistake," he murmured, hanging his head. "It was not for horses. It was grain that the colonel bought from me. Horses—he bought horses before—at an earlier time."

"You're a liar, Coronel!" Bannock snapped. "And so are you, Mantavo. Both of you are lying through your teeth. This money"—Bannock held up the cash"—this was a bribe the colonel paid you, Coronel. A bribe to keep quiet about what you knew he was doing. Namely, rustling and then selling stolen cattle." Bannock threw the money on the ground and watched as Coronel stared longingly at it. "How often do you pay for the *alcalde*'s beneficial silence? Weekly? Monthly?

"You are a most obnoxious man, Mr. Bannock," Mantavo said icily. "In my country we have ways of dealing with such men. Ways you would not at all like, I can assure you. Why do you not go away now, Mr. Bannock? I am willing to forget that this conversation ever took place if you are."

"And I am willing to forgive you for coming here today," Coronel said quickly, "and casting a pall over my Magdalena's party."

"I don't want nor do I need your forgetting, Mantavo, or your forgiveness, Coronel," Bannock countered. "What I want and need is the truth—and justice."

With that he strode over to the carriage where Diego Anza was seated, watching Bannock's encounter with the two Mexicans with avid interest.

"You," Bannock said, jabbing a finger in Anza's direction. "Do you remember me?"

"No, señor, I do not remember you," Anza replied placidly. "That is because I have never seen you before in my life."

"You're going to sit there and deny that you tried to rustle some cattle up north? That me and two other fellows ran you off and killed the man with you? That one of you shot and killed one of us?"

Bannock described the location of the meeting, concluding with, "It was south of the Nueces River and my spread."

Anza's eyes shifted from Bannock to his employer, who had come up alongside the carriage. "Colonel," he complained, "this man says I am a rustler. That he has seen me stealing cows from the *gringos*. Yet I do not know him and I am not guilty of what he says I do."

"Pay no attention to him," Mantavo advised Anza. "The man suffers perhaps from too much sun." He climbed into the carriage and seated himself next to his driver. Looking down at Bannock, he said, "I cannot say I am glad we met, but I can say I am glad that we will probably never see one another again."

"Don't be too sure about that, Colonel. We may very well meet again. If and when we do, as seems likely to me at the moment, the time for polite words and dancing around each other will be over. Then it will be time for action—for settling this problem once and for all.

"Meanwhile, I'll give you fair warning. I mean to leave no stone unturned to stop you and Anza and the rest of your border bandits. I'll do whatever I have to to see that your rustling comes to a halt."

"How do you propose to stop me, Mr. Bannock? Mind you now—I am not admitting to anything. I am merely morbidly fascinated by you and your wild words as one always is in the presence of a clear case of madness."

"You must think I'm a bad poker player, Colonel. I assure you I am not. I don't let on what high cards I'm holding until I'm ready to play them."

"You speak of poker and your skill at the game. I suspect your skill lies principally in bluffing as practiced by so many poker players."

"Time will tell whether I'm bluffing or not, won't it? Maybe American justice can do what Mexican justice won't do." Bannock glanced pointedly at the bribe money lying on the ground in the distance and then at Coronel, who was standing near it while trying and failing to appear totally uninterested in it.

"There is an old saying in my country, Mr. Bannock. 'Trouble comes running to those who court it.' Drive, Diego."

Bannock stood watching as the carriage pulled away. Fury seethed within him but it did not show on his virtually expressionless face as Mantavo's warning words echoed in his mind.

SIX

BANNOCK ARRIVED HOME two days later and was met at the railroad station by Wes Holbrook.

"Got your telegraph message, boss," Holbrook declared as he loaded Bannock's carpetbag into the rear of the spring wagon he had driven into town.

"I see you're hard at it," Bannock commented as he climbed up on the driver's seat and Holbrook did the same. He indicated with a nod the rolls of barbed wire piled in the bed of the wagon.

"We have been ever since you left, Mr. Bannock. We've got almost thirty-one miles fenced in already and the boys are working on another eight or nine miles right this very minute."

"What about the extra men? Did you find any worth hiring?"

"Two all told. They're both good men and handy with a gun. I've put the word out around town that we could use a few more men. Maybe some will show up before long. The guard tower at the main house is going up but there's still a lot of work that remains to be done on it. I've got men riding the fence in shifts twenty-four hours a day."

"Sounds like things are progressing satisfactorily. Have you had any trouble while I was gone?"

"No, sir. Everything's been about as peaceful as a baby cured of the colic, I'm happy to be able to say. I took that draft you gave me over to Tom Butler and me and some of the boys brought the cattle you bought from him back to our range. How about you, boss? Did you get what you went after down south?"

"I'm afraid not. All I got for my trouble was a pack of lies from Colonel Mantavo and the runaround from the mayor of Matamoros, who, it turns out, is being paid off by Mantavo to keep out of his way."

"You couldn't pin Mantavo down, is that it?"

"He wouldn't admit the sun was shining on a day without a cloud in the sky, never mind admitting that he's been running a rustling ring. I don't know how many other officials besides the mayor of Matamoros he's been paying off to let him have a free hand with Texas cattle. Probably a goodly number of them. There's no way he could operate as successfully as he does, I'm convinced, without having to grease more than a few palms."

"Did you tell him about what happened to Josh Cameron?"

"I did. What's more, I found myself face to face with one of the two men who were raiding Tom Butler's stock that day. I confronted the man with what I knew—what had happened— and he just up and denied he knew anything at all about what I was saying. He claimed, the scar-faced bastard did, that he never laid eyes on me in my life. A pretty hard thing to do considering as how he almost left me minus one ear as a result of our little encounter."

"How do things stand now then?"

"About the same way they did before I went down south. I couldn't get the Matamoros law to help me. Mantavo has bought and paid for that in the person of the mayor, a man named Xavier Coronel. Mantavo denies everything although he tended to taunt me some about the matter. He sort of let on he's done what I know damn well he has but then he skidded out and away from it without flat-out admitting he's ever done anything more serious than missing Sunday school at the local mission."

"It sounds to me then," Holbrook mused, "that we're right back where we started from. Which is not the best place in the world to be right now."

"That's about the long and the short of it, Wes, I'm truly sorry to say. I did what I could but I didn't win any prizes down there."

"Well, things aren't all black as the pit," Holbrook declared more cheerfully. "Like I said, the fence is going up fast. So's the guard tower. We got two more guns on our side now than we had before you left. If push comes to shove one of these days, we'll likely be able to hold our own."

"You're to be congratulated on a job well done, Wes. So don't take what I'm fixing to say the wrong way. I'm not content with just being able to hold our own. I want to go on the attack."

"Where? When?"

"I don't know yet. But the way I see it, if we don't stand up on our hind legs and go after those Mexicans, they're going to be all over us before long. We won't have enough cattle left to make it worthwhile driving them to Kansas if those rustlers keep at it the way they've been going. A ranch like this—I could be put out of business in less time than it takes to tally up the place's losses."

The discussion ended when they reached the ranch, where Bannock got down from the wagon. Carrying his carpetbag, he bade farewell to Holbrook and went inside. The first thing he did, even before he unpacked or took the bath he so much wanted, was to sit down at his desk and compose telegraph messages he intended to send to the governor of Texas in Austin, to the state's two senators and to its representatives in Washington, D.C. In them, he stated the problems the ranchers in southern Texas were facing from Mexican rustling and listed the accompanying atrocities that he knew about. He ended his messages with a fervent plea for help. Only then did he permit himself the luxury of a bath.

As he scrubbed himself, he thought about the task facing him. It was, he realized, a daunting one. But one he was nevertheless determined to undertake. To avoid it would mean personal and professional disaster. No, he had, as he saw it, no choice but to continue his struggle to stop the depredations of the raiders and stop them as soon as possible.

He glanced at the messages he had written and would send on the following morning. They might bring the needed help he and the other ranchers in the area so desperately needed. He refused to let himself consider the possibility—a very real one, he knew—that his messages would fall, if not on deaf ears, at least on unalarmed ears unable or unwilling to respond.

That night when he went to bed he dreamed of a plague of Diego Anza-faced locusts that descended upon the land and destroyed it utterly to the vast amusement of Mantavo, the locusts' leader. Bannock fought them with fire, sword and gun until the dream finally ended as did the night. But when Bannock arose in the morning and stretched he knew, remembering the dream that was more nightmare than dream, that the battle had not ended. It had merely entered a new phase.

The following morning after breakfast, Bannock sent one of his men into town with the telegraph messages he had prepared and then saddled his bay and rode out, following the newly installed fence which eventually led him to where his men were working at extending the barbed barrier. He dismounted and joined them, working side by side with Viviano Colorado as both men dug deep postholes.

"If the bandits do not kill us, boss," a grinning Viviano declared, "this work will break our backs. We will lie here in the hot sun and serve as supper for the vultures."

"You know something, Viviano, I think you're right as rain," Bannock, also grinning, said as he slammed his shovel into the hard-packed earth and tossed clods and loose dirt over his shoulder.

It was, as Viviano had said, back-breaking work. But Bannock did it with a vengeance, not allowing his aching muscles or sweat-blinded eyes to slow his furious pace. He stopped only for a few minutes to straighten up and press his fingers into the small of his back to ease the pain that had come to nest and gnaw at him there.

The sound of nine-pound sledges filled the air as the men

placing the posts in position moved along behind the diggers of the holes. The pounding was accompanied by the occasional curse of a fence-stringer who had cut himself on the fence's wire barbs and by the metallic clipping of lengths of fence as they were nailed securely into place on the posts.

"Come and get!" the cook called out at almost the precise moment the sun reached its meridian.

Bannock and his ranch hands dropped their shovels and other tools and headed, most of them walking stiffly, to where the chuck wagon sat in the shade of two tall yellow pines.

Bannock took a plate and lined up with his men. As the cook placed a thick mixture of rice and pinto beans on his plate, he helped himself to a warm pair of buttered biscuits. He was hungrily eating when two men rode into camp from different directions—two men he had never seen before.

Wes Holbrook, hunkered down not far from the chuck wagon, rose and called out a greeting to them. Then he beckoned and they followed him over to where Bannock was standing with his plate in one hand and a fork in the other.

"Boss," he said, "these are the two men I hired. Meet Sam Cavendish and Milo Hunter."

Cavendish was a gaunt man with a body made more of bones than flesh. His eyes were set deep in his head and they seemed to glitter as he leaned down and shook hands with Bannock. Hunter was the opposite of Cavendish—round as a barrel, with eyes that were mild and filled with what might have been mistaken for innocence. But Bannock noticed the notches carved in the grips of Hunter's six-guns that hung heavy on his hip. The man didn't bother to shake hands.

"Wes had good things to say about you boys," Bannock remarked. "Glad to have you with us."

"We got the impression," Hunter drawled, "that we could expect to see some action when we hired on here, Mr. Bannock. But so far all we've seen is cows and more cows. Not a single desperado in sight."

"That's good news as far as I'm concerned," Bannock said. "I'm not keen on shooting at folks. Nor am I keen on killing—"

"Then how come your foreman hired us?" Cavendish asked as he switched his toothpick from one side of his mouth to the other.

"Don't misunderstand me, Cavendish. The fact that I don't go looking for a shooting war with anybody doesn't mean that I won't join one if somebody else starts it."

"We were told a bunch of greasers are giving ranchers round here a headache or two now and then," Hunter prompted.

"What Wes told you's true," Bannock said, forking food into his mouth. "There've been some pretty ugly incidents." He told the two men about the torture and murder of Phil McIntyre and his wife, Amelia, and about the killing of Josh Cameron.

"Those greasers, should they show up here where they're not wanted, well, we know how to handle them," Cavendish commented laconically.

"Hunter and Cavendish have been riding patrol, boss," Holbrook explained.

"We just met up," Hunter said, "and decided to ride in and make our nooning."

"Together?" Bannock asked in a neutral tone.

The two men looked at one another and then back at Bannock.

"Do you think that's a good idea?" he asked them. "The two of you coming in together with nobody left out there to ride patrol?"

"It was as quiet out there as a church on a Saturday night," a peevish Cavendish commented. "So we came in."

"Maybe it was quiet because you were both out there. I suggest that one of you continue patrolling until the other one finishes eating. Then he can spell you. You decide which one of you gets to eat first."

The two men conversed in low voices and then Hunter wheeled his mount and headed back the way he had come.

Cavendish dismounted and took up a position at the end of the chow line.

Bannock handed his empty plate to the cook and poured himself a cup of coffee. He hunkered down and sipped the black brew in silence as Holbrook left him and went to lend a hand to the men who were unloading barbed wire from a wagon that had just pulled into camp.

He was finishing the last of his coffee when the first shot sounded. It struck the cook's Dutch oven but missed the ranch hand who was sitting cross-legged on the ground next to it. The shot was immediately followed by others—an intense volley of them.

One of the hands let out a yell and then an angry epithet as he was hit. The shot spun him around and hurled him against the side of the chuck wagon.

Bannock leaped to his feet, tossing away his coffee cup and going for his gun as Hunter rode back into camp, pursued by a band of mounted riders who, as he leaped from his saddle and took refuge behind the chuck wagon, began to fire at Bannock and his men, who were running for any kind of cover they could find.

Bannock dropped down behind a small boulder which afforded him protection only when he bellied down on the ground. The first shot he fired nicked one of the Mexicans in the thigh and forced the man to retreat to the cover of a stand of post oaks.

Viviano Colorado, crouching behind the chuck wagon not far from Bannock yelled, *"Cuidado!"* and Bannock did indeed "look out" as a Mexican, his mount rearing, squeezed off a shot in his direction. He scuttled along the ground so that the boulder that was serving him as a stony breastwork was between him and his assailant. The man's round bit into the boulder, sending up a thin spray of stone dust. Bannock returned the fire, hitting the man's horse, which threw its rider and then went down to thrash helplessly on the ground as the life flowed from it along with its blood.

Cursing in Spanish, the unhorsed man ran toward one of his mounted companions and leaped up behind him.

The man was, Bannock realized, none other than Diego Anza!

Anza, fighting for control of his horse, fired a single shot that went whining over Bannock's head. Before Bannock could return the fire, Anza went galloping away toward a stand of young mesquite trees in the distance. When he reached them, he quickly dismounted. So did the man riding behind him. Both of them took up positions behind the trunks of two mesquite trees. With barely a pause, they continued firing at Bannock and the men in the camp they had pinned down in the camp with him.

"Ben Bannock!" Anza bellowed. "We have come here to teach you a lesson. Give yourself up to us and your men will not be hurt."

When Bannock did not respond, one of Anza's men fired several shots in rapid succession from a carbine. They went *pinging* under the chuck wagon and two of them slammed into Milo Hunter, who went flying backward. His gun fell from his hand as he hit the ground several feet away from where he had been crouching and he did not move except for a slow twisting of his right leg. In a moment, that too was still.

The sound of gunfire was deafening and Bannock almost choked on the gunsmoke that was filling the air with the stench of spent powder. He scouted the area, picking his targets carefully, firing only when he thought he had a good chance of hitting one of the attackers. But they were wily and he managed to wound only one of them.

When the hammer of his pistol clicked on an empty chamber, he shifted position and reloaded as fast as he could, thumbing cartridges out of his belt and filling the chambers of his gun, the barrel of which was now warm.

He resumed his former position and also resumed firing—at Diego Anza. The man was clearly the leader of the raiders. If he could take him out of action . . .

He squinted down the barrel of his gun, squeezed the trigger . . .

But he did not fire. Because suddenly Anza was nowhere in sight. Bannock wasn't sure if he was still behind one of the mesquite trees. He waited, hoping to catch a glimpse of Anza, gunsmoke filling his nostrils and making him want to sneeze.

He didn't have to wait long. Anza ducked out from behind the tree, fired a round, ducked back again.

"Got one!"

It had been Wes Holbrook who had given the triumphant yell, Bannock realized, as one of the Mexicans who was crouching behind his horse fell to the ground, clutching his ankle which had been shattered by Holbrook's shot.

Holbrook fired again. The foreman's second shot caught the Mexican in the chest as the man tried to crawl away to the cover of some broken boulders. The Mexican's body bounced along the ground with the impact of the round that had plowed into his body.

The foreman raised the barrel of his gun, blew away the smoke emerging from it and gave Bannock a victorious grin.

"Look out!" Bannock yelled. But his warning came an instant too late.

A Mexican stepped out from behind a tree and fired. His shot blew the top of Holbrook's head off.

A cold hand gripped and twisted Bannock's gut as his foreman and friend went down without a sound and lay there on the ground, eyes staring up at the sun he would never see again.

"Señor Bannock!"

It was Anza who had called out.

"How many men will you lose before you surrender yourself to us?" the scar-faced raider shouted from the relative safety of his position behind the mesquite tree.

"We came here for you, Señor Bannock. Your men do not have to die. It is you who makes much trouble for Colonel Mantavo.

"You *vaqueros!*" Anza shouted, addressing Bannock's men. "We do not wish your deaths. Go away. Leave Señor Bannock to us."

Anza's plea was met by a deafening round of fire from Bannock's men, which lifted his heart and strengthened his desire to defeat Anza and his bandits. He too fired.

One of the Mexicans screamed. Then, silence.

Bannock leaped to his feet and, rallying his men with a shout and a wave of his gun hand, raced toward the chuck wagon.

"We'll use it to cover a frontal attack," Bannock told them. "We'll also use it as a battering ram to try to send those Mexicans high-tailing it out of here."

Viviano Colorado slammed shut the chuck box and put his shoulder against it.

"Aim for Anza!" Bannock yelled, and pointed out the ringleader's position. "We'll push the wagon," he yelled. "The rest of you men stay close behind us so you don't get your you-know-whats shot off. Let's *roll!*"

The chuck wagon groaned and creaked into life as Bannock and Colorado shouldered it toward the Mexicans' ragged skirmish line. It began to rumble and then to rattle as it careened toward the Mexicans, who began frantically firing in a futile attempt to hit the men clustered cautiously behind it.

"When we get to where we're going," a nearly out-of-breath Bannock managed to yell, "fan out and roust the bastards!"

The chuck wagon lurched dangerously from side to side, constantly threatening to overturn, as it sped toward the trees in the distance. The men pushing it never let up for a moment. The water barrel lashed to the side of the wagon lost its cover and water went sloshing out of it, making the ground underfoot treacherous. But Bannock and the others remained upright as gunfire erupted all around and above them.

Then Bannock gave the signal. He and Colorado let the wagon go. And go it did. It careened along the rough ground, tilting crazily from side to side, but moving ever onward.

The men ran behind it and then fanned out firing as Bannock had ordered.

As the chuck wagon crashed into the mesquite tree behind which Anza had taken cover, the Mexican let out a yell of frustration and then began to back off, shouting to his men to do the same.

As Bannock's attack continued, the Mexicans turned and fled for their horses. One of them, who did not move swiftly enough, went down with more than one man's bullet in his body.

Bannock ducked a flying stave from the shattered water barrel which came flying through the air toward him from the wrecked chuck wagon and fired at Anza. But his shot was too high.

Before he could fire again, Anza was aboard his horse and galloping south. Ahead of him rode the remainder of his men who had survived the gunfight.

"We did it, boss!" Viviano crowed, tossing his hat and firing a shot into the air. "They are in Old Mexico by now, you bet!" Another happy shot.

The only sign now of the Mexican presence were the clouds of dust laced with grains of sand that the fleeing men had left behind them.

Bannock looked about him. At the dead horse some distance away. At the dead bodies of several Mexicans sprawled in grotesque positions on the ground. At the corpses of Milo Hunter and Wes Holbrook.

"*Madre de Dios!*" Viviano Colorado exclaimed as he took off his hat and stood bareheaded in the hot sun. "This place, it looks like a slaughterhouse." He crossed himself and murmured a soft prayer.

"Viviano, I want you to do something for me," Bannock said, staring at Holbrook's body.

"I do whatever it is you want, boss."

"From now on I want you to be the foreman of this ranch and trail boss when we drive our cattle up to Kansas to sell."

Viviano almost dropped his hat. He stared at Bannock, the traces of a smile flickering about his lips. But then, apparently realizing that Bannock was not joking, he sobered and said, "I can do it, boss. I *will* do it. You will not be sorry you have made me foreman."

"But you might be sorry, Viviano."

"Boss?"

"Those bastards will be back. You can count on that. Sooner or later, they'll be back. You might not be so lucky next time. Next time it might be you lying there dead as a doornail."

Viviano's gaze shifted to the bodies littering the ground. "The world, boss, it is a dangerous place. But I can't help myself. I like living in it. I will like living in it even more now that I am foreman of the Bannock ranch."

When Bannock saw pride in Viviano's eyes—and something else—courage, he knew he had chosen the right man for the job Wes Holbrook could now no longer do.

"Listen up, men!" he called out to gain the attention of his ranch hands. "I've just appointed Viviano Colorado ranch foreman and trail boss. He'll be giving the orders from now on and I hope you'll have no trouble taking them. I say that because I know a lot of you—especially after what's happened here today —don't have altogether kindly feelings toward Mexicans. And Viviano, as you all well know, is a Mexican.

"He's also something else. He's a true and faithful friend who's been with me for more than eight years. In fact, he was the second man I hired when I was just starting to build my spread. Wes Holbrook, may he rest in everlasting peace, was the first. I trust Viviano. So can you.

"But, if any of you think you'll have any problems working under his orders, come on back to the house with me. I'll pay you off and you can ride out with no hard feelings on my part."

Bannock waited. None of the men took him up on his offer. Instead, several of them went up to Viviano and shook his hand as they congratulated him on his promotion.

The relief Bannock felt at their show of support for his decision was evident on his face. "The first thing we've got to do," he told the men, "is bury the dead. I'd lend you a hand but I'm leaving."

"Where you headed, boss?" one of the men inquired.

"I'm riding out after those bandits."

"We'll go with you," the ranch hand who had just spoken volunteered. "All of us will. Right, boys?"

A cheer of assent went up from Bannock's men.

He held up his hand for quiet. "I appreciate the offer, I truly do. But I need you fellows to stay right here and protect the ranch and the stock. I don't know exactly when I'll be back. But I'll keep in touch with Viviano and he'll keep you posted."

Then, when the men had picked up the shovels they had earlier been using to dig postholes and had begun to use them to dig graves, Bannock turned to Viviano. "Your pay is raised 50 percent as of now."

"*Gracias,* boss. Now I will be able to buy all the chili peppers I want. Even a wicked woman now and then."

Bannock matched his new foreman's grin. "You'll be in charge here while I'm gone, Viviano. See to it that the guard tower is finished as fast as possible and manned twenty-four hours a day. Tell the hands I'll pay each one of them a fifty-dollar bonus if they get the rest of the fence up in no more than two days from now."

Viviano walked with Bannock as he headed for his horse. "Take good care of yourself, boss," he said, and reverently added *"Vaya con Dios,"* as Bannock swung into the saddle and moved his horse out, heading south—the way Anza and the rest of the brush-riders had gone.

The trail was hot and Bannock followed it easily. How many men was he trailing? He wasn't sure. Three? Four? More? He tried to remember the gunfight in detail to determine how many Mexicans had been killed and, thus, how many were riding up ahead of him. He finally had to give it up. All he could clearly recall was gunfire and blood and the deaths of Wes Holbrook and Milo Hunter.

So he concentrated even more closely on the tracks the bandits' horses had left behind them. When he came to a sandy stretch of ground, the bunched tracks spread out and he was

finally able to see clearly that he was after four men, one of them
Diego Anza.

The name and the image of the man's scarred face enraged
him. Easy, he silently told himself. Save your anger and your lust
for revenge for when it will be needed. For when you've finally
run your quarry to ground. Then both his anger and hate, he
knew, would serve him well in the showdown that was coming.

The Mexicans' trail led south in almost a straight line except
for one side excursion to water the horses and themselves no
doubt. But they didn't stay at the waterhole they had found very
long. The horses had left behind muddy footprints on the bank
but not as many as they would have had they lingered. They're
running and running hard, Bannock thought. So they didn't let
their mounts take in too much water. Maybe they've spotted me.
There was that hill back there. They could have seen me from its
crest as I came across the tableland north of it.

But he had not seen them although his eyes had been—and
still were—straining for a glimpse of them.

The trail led him around a bend and to a shallow stream that
was flowing from east to west. He recognized it as a tributary of
the larger stream where Anza and the others had paused to
water their horses. The bandits' tracks led into the water. But
not out of it on the opposite side.

Bannock drew rein and sat his saddle, scanning the area in
both directions. From his position, he could see no spot where
the riders had emerged from the water.

What now? He turned his bay and rode along the northern
bank of the stream, heading west, his eyes on the ground before
him. He knew that most men who ride water will come out on
the same side that they went in. But still he saw no sign of
anyone having emerged from the stream.

He halted and studied the stream bed itself. He saw no overturned stones lying in it and no sign that the men had ridden
this way. Usually, he knew, a good tracker could find traces of a
horse and rider's passage through water. A dislodged stone.
Hoofprints not yet smoothed out by the flowing water. But here

there was nothing like that, nothing at all that was of any help to him.

He wheeled his mount and trotted back the way he had come. As he passed the point where he had started, he kept his eyes peeled for sign of the bandits having left the water on either side of the stream. Still nothing.

But then, several minutes later, he saw the stretch of stirred-up dirt on the opposite side of the stream. There were wavy patterns in it that did not match the dirt on either side of it. He rode into the water and then out of it. A tree branch, he thought. One of the men he was trailing had used a leafy tree branch to try to cover up the tracks he and the men with him were making.

Bannock smiled. All he had to do now was follow the trail the men had left, which was plain to him despite their efforts to hide it, and he would once again be on the trail of his prey. The fact that he had lost time riding the stream's bank bothered him but he had done what he had had to do.

He swore under his breath as the trail led him to a vast stretch of rocky ground that reached to some hills near the horizon. The brush marks in the dirt ended where the rocks began. He walked his horse out onto the rocks. The animal's footing became immediately unsteady. But of more concern to Bannock was the fact that he could no longer discern any trace of the raiders' trail.

He swore again and rode across the rocky ground, searching in vain for some sign, however slight it might be, of the men he was hunting. When he found none, he stood up in his stirrups and, pulling his hat down low on his forehead to keep the sun out of his eyes, scanned the land as far as he could see ahead of and on both sides of him.

To the east was a small dwelling with smoke coming from a stone chimney. He headed for it. Once he reached it, he drew rein and hallooed the house that was little more than a shack.

A man wearing the loose-fitting white cotton garments of the Mexican peasantry emerged from the building to stand peering up at him.

"Good day," he greeted the man. "I'm looking for four riders that I think might have come this way. Have you by any chance seen them?"

The man responded in Spanish slow enough for Bannock to be able to make out a few words. He nodded his head and pointed to the east.

Yes, the man was saying, four riders had come by his rancho and had ridden east.

"Did one of them have a scar on his face? Here?" Bannock touched his forehead.

"*Sí.*" The Mexican touched his own forehead and nodded vigorously. Again he pointed to the east.

"*Muchas gracias.*" Bannock rode away, heading east.

An hour later he had still found no sign of his quarry. But he did come upon another rancho—a ramshackle building with a tarpaper roof, actually—where a plump Mexican woman was seated on a wooden milking stool as she shelled peas beside her overgrown garden and two nanny goats constantly tried to get at her pea-filled bowl.

Bannock again asked his questions and again he was told that yes, the woman had seen the men he was looking for. They had turned south.

Was she sure?

Yes, she was very sure.

Bannock rode south, leaving the woman to her peas and goats.

Some time later, he rode into the small town of Pecos without having caught so much as a glimpse of Anza and his men. The town consisted of a main street lined with adobe buildings—a cantina, a general store, a livery, a tin shop, a bootmaker. Its citizens, as far as Bannock could see, were mostly Mexicans although he did notice one Anglo standing in front of the livery.

He dismounted, tied his bay to a hitch rail and went into the cantina where he ordered whiskey from the short Mexican behind the bar. When he had a bottle and glass in front of him, he asked if the man had seen Anza and the three men riding with him.

The Mexican shook his head, averting his eyes from Bannock.

"I'm not the law," Bannock said. "Those men are friends of mine," he lied.

The Mexican's eyes flickered in his direction and then darted away again.

Bannock laid a gold eagle on the wet surface of the bar.

The Mexican seemed transfixed by it. He looked up at Bannock.

"The name of man with the scar on his forehead is Diego Anza," Bannock said, pushing the gold coin in the bar dog's direction but keeping his finger on it. "It's important that I find him."

"*Amigo?*"

"*Sí,* like I just told you, Anza's a friend of mine," Bannock lied again.

The bar dog sighed. He looked away from Bannock and the coin. "I do not know nothing, señor. I cannot help you find your friend."

As the man turned away to wait on another customer, Bannock regretfully pocketed the gold eagle and poured himself a drink. He drank a silent toast to failure.

After he had downed and paid for his drink, he left the cantina and, being unable to give up, went across the street to the livery where the Anglo man he had noticed earlier still lounged.

"Howdy," he greeted the man. "Maybe you can help me."

"With what?"

"I'm looking for some men. Some Mexican men."

The American shifted his weight from one foot to the other, waiting.

"One of them has a scar on his forehead."

"Diego Anza," said the man before Bannock could say anything more.

"You know him?"

"Not personally. But I know about him."

"Would you happen to know where he is at the moment?"

Bannock asked, forcing his voice to remain level and suppressing the sense of excitement that was surging within him.

"Nope."

Bannock's hopes sank.

"But I know where he was, if that's of any help."

"Where he was?"

"Anza and his bad boys raided a horse ranch northwest of here earlier today. Heard about it from a livery barn bum that was out that way when the raid happened. Anza had three men with him, according to this fella who told me about the raid. They got away with a goodly number of horses."

"This happened earlier today, you say?"

"That's what I was told."

Bannock recalled the Mexican man he had spoken to previously who had told him that he had seen Anza and the three men with him riding due east. He thought of the pea-shelling woman and her goats who had also, apparently, deliberately misdirected him.

"You after Anza?" the livery barn lounger asked.

"I am. He raided my ranch. Killed two of my men. I've been asking around after him but people have been sending me on wild goose chases."

"I take it the people you asked were Mexicans."

Bannock nodded.

"Mister, you keep on asking greasers where to find Anza and you'll still be asking them come the Last Trump. No greaser's gonna tell you anything about Anza or his boss."

"Colonel Mantavo."

"Him. One's as bad as the other. They're a hell-bred pair that were made for each other, from what I hear tell."

"Why do you say no Mexican will steer me in Anza's direction?"

"Too scared, that's why. If any Mex turns on any of the men who ride for Mantavo, they'll wind up dead and their dying will take a real long time and not be very nice from what I hear. Mantavo and Anza, they've got the greasers all around here on both sides of the border whipped into line. None of them will admit to knowing a damn thing about those fellas."

"From what I've experienced, I'd have to say you're right."

"I know I'm right. I've been drifting through these parts since spring. I've heard how things are and seen the lay of the land. You're wasting your time, mister, if you don't mind my saying so. Unless maybe you can get Franco Flores to lend you a hand in your hunt."

"Franco Flores? Who's he?"

"Used to be the *alcalde* down in Matamoros. But Mantavo saw to it that things got hot for old Flores. So hot the man had to resign in the end or wind up dead. He's no coward, is Flores, but he had a young granddaughter to look out for since her parents died in the cholera outbreak they had down around Brownsville a couple of years ago. I reckon he figured if Mantavo did him in who'd look out for his granddaughter. So he threw in the towel. He quit his job and moved north across the border. He lives north of Brownsville now with his granddaughter. He might be able and willing to help you."

"I appreciate the information. It does begin to look to me as though I've got to get somebody on my side else I'll never run Anza and the rest of his gang to ground. I think I'll head on down toward Brownsville. Have myself a talk with this Flores fellow. Maybe he'll be willing to help me out."

"Mister, don't take no offense but I got to say I think you're either a fool or a gunslick. Only one or the other would dare have a go at taking down Anza or any of his ilk. They're real good with guns and they don't give a hoot in a holler who or how many they have to kill to get whatever they happen to want at any given time."

"I'm neither a fool nor a gunslick," Bannock said thoughtfully. "I'm just a man who, if somebody steps on his toes, won't rest easy till he gets even."

"Well, all I can say to you is good luck. You're going to need a bushel or two of it if and when you come face to face with Diego Anza or Colonel Mantavo."

SEVEN

EARLY THE FOLLOWING MORNING, Bannock went to his saddlebag and took out some bread he had bought before leaving Pecos. He hunkered down beside his campfire to eat it, washing it down with water from his canteen. When the bread was gone, he rose and went over to where his hobbled horse was browsing. He checked the animal's shoes and was glad to find that they were all firmly in place. He shook out his saddle blanket, which he had hung over the limb of a cottonwood the night before, and found it to be as dry as a bone. He folded it once and then draped it over the back of his bay.

Within minutes, he had the animal saddled and bridled. He removed the hobbles from its front legs and stored them in his saddlebag. Leading his horse, he returned to his fire, kicked it out and then put a foot in a stirrup and stepped into the saddle. He rode away from the camp, heading toward Brownsville in the distance.

Later that morning, as he neared the town, he stopped at a small rancho where several dark-skinned children were playing some sort of game that entailed dashing in and out of a colorful stand of hollyhocks where bees buzzed but seemed not to bother the game players.

Using his rudimentary Spanish, he inquired about the location of the Flores ranch. The children told him where to find it

and then stood watching as the Anglo stranger touched the
brim of his hat to them and rode away.

Following the directions he had been given, Bannock found
the rancho with little difficulty. It was located due north of
Brownsville. It nestled against the sloping side of a hill that
served as a windbreak as did the tall pines planted on either side
of it. It was built of adobe, was a single story tall and covered a
good fifteen hundred square feet of ground, Bannock estimated. A modest but more than adequate structure.

A shed behind it was sturdily built of timbers and through its
open door, Bannock could see an old man moving about and
speaking softly in Spanish although no one else was visible from
Bannock's vantage point.

The man had a dark complexion and eyes, which contrasted
sharply with a thick mane of hair as white as milk. The skin of his
face was lined with age but the lines did not detract significantly
from the rugged handsomeness of his features. He moved with
an elegant combination of grace and strength.

Bannock rode around the side of the house and halted a few
yards from the entrance to the shed where he called out to the
man within.

The Mexican halted and stared out at Bannock for a moment
before leaving the shed and emerging into the bright sunshine.

"Señor, there is something I can do for you?"

The old man greets strangers graciously, Bannock thought
before replying, "Are you by any chance Franco Flores?"

"Sí, señor. That is my name."

"Mine's Ben Bannock, Señor Flores. I've come to have a talk
with you about something that's important to me."

Bannock saw the look of puzzlement come over Flores's face
as he stared up at his visitor. Bannock explained, "I'm a rancher
from up near the Nueces River, Señor Flores. I've been having
some trouble with Mexican raiders and thought— Would you
mind if I stepped down?"

Flores shook his head slightly as if recovering from a daydream. "I forget my manners. Please. Step down from your saddle, Mr. Bannock, and we will talk."

As Bannock dismounted, Flores said, "But first—I must see to Esmeralda. She is not feeling well. Would you like to come inside the shed with me or wait out here until I am finished?"

"I'll come inside with you."

Once in the shed, Bannock was surprised to find that Esmeralda was not a woman, as he had assumed, but a cow.

"Esmeralda has lump jaw," Flores declared, taking a bottle down from a wooden shelf. "I go yesterday to Brownsville. There the druggist gives me this." He held up a bottle. "He says this will cure my Esmeralda."

"That stuff works," Bannock said, nodding at the bottle of Fleming's Lump Jaw Cure in Flores's hand. "I've used it and it works fine nine times out of ten."

"Ah, that is good to hear." Flores entered the stall where he had penned his cow, poured some of the contents out of the bottle into his hand and began to rub it gently on Esmeralda's badly swollen jaw.

The cow lowed and pulled her head away.

"Now, now, Esmeralda," Flores crooned soothingly.

But the cow continued to resist his attempts to treat her until Bannock entered the stall on the opposite side from where Flores was standing and got a firm grip on the cow's head. He held it steady as Flores continued his treatment.

"Esmeralda gives good milk," Flores said. "I trust her infection will go away. Cows are expensive these days. But, besides the expense—I would miss the old girl if she were to die. She and I have become friends over the years. Ever since the day she finally stopped trying to kick me when I tried to milk her even though her bag was full and she was very much in need of relief."

Bannock's smile matched the one on Flores's face. Bannock held on to Esmeralda while Flores continued to apply some of the bottle's contents to the animal's jaw. He released the cow only when Flores signaled that he had finished the task.

Then, after replacing the bottle of ointment on the shelf, Flores accompanied Bannock out of the shed into the day that had begun to become cloudy.

"Come, señor, we will go into the house. There we will talk."

Bannock followed the old man into the relatively cool interior of the adobe building and took the chair in the main room that Flores directed him to. The old man sat down opposite him, folded his hands in his lap, and said, "You spoke of raids across the border, Señor Bannock."

"Yes, I did. There have been many. My own men and myself were attacked only yesterday by men associated with a man named Pedro Mantavo."

Something glittered in Flores's eyes like the embers of a banked fire suddenly flaring into unexpected life.

"You know him?"

"I know him. He is a very powerful man in Mexico. He is not a man to—how say you Americans—to tangle with?"

"I've tangled with him in the persons of some of the men who ride for him. I managed to catch some of Mantavo's bandits and they're in jail right now. Yesterday I ran another bunch off my spread. That time they were led by a man I understand is close to Mantavo. A man named—"

"Diego Anza."

Bannock nodded. "I rode down into Mexico—Matamoros— to have a talk with the law there—with the *alcalde* of Matamoros —Xavier Coronel. I thought maybe I could get him to put some judicial pressure on Mantavo. Maybe get Mantavo to back off some if not to actually stop his rustling altogether. But—"

"But you were not successful."

"No, I'm sorry to say I was not. You don't seem surprised at that."

"I am not. I know Señor Coronel is a colleague of Mantavo's although that is a secret nearly everyone on both sides of the border knows but no one will admit to knowing."

"When I was at Coronel's place, I found out more or less by accident that Mantavo is paying him bribes to let him operate without any legal problems. I've since heard that you and Mantavo have locked horns in the past."

"What exactly have you heard in that regard, Señor Bannock?"

"I met a fella who told me you used to be the mayor of Matamoros. The fella I met, he said Mantavo put the pressure on you when you tried to interfere with what he was up to. The fella said you had to resign to protect yourself and your granddaughter."

"*Sí,* I resigned. But it was for Celia's sake, not mine. I am an old man, as you can see, Señor Bannock. I have not many years left to live. But Celia, my granddaughter, she is young. Only twenty. I did not want anything to happen to her. So when Mantavo spoke privately to me of the joys of retirement, as you Americans call it, I listened. Soon afterward, I quit my job and moved with Celia to this place to be away from the past and the ghosts that haunt it. It is easy for a man to be brave when it is only himself he must worry about. But then things change. He is no longer alone. He must think not only of himself but of others."

"Your granddaughter."

Flores nodded. "Celia is cursed."

"I beg your pardon?"

"Celia is both young and beautiful and that in some places at some times makes a woman doubly cursed. Of course, as time passes, she will no longer be young or beautiful and thus her cursed state will give way at last to a blessed one of peace and contentment. The raging river in her blood will have run dry and will not drive her to foolish acts and excesses. Celia finds Colonel Mantavo attractive. To her, he is a cavalier. Dashing and romantic.

"I have told her repeatedly that he is a man to be avoided as one avoids a snake one knows to be poisonous. But she will not listen to me. She is strongly attracted to him. Señor Bannock, I tell you with both regret and fear in my heart that hers is the attraction of the moth for the prettily flickering flame."

"Does she know about his rustling?"

"I have told her. She refuses to believe me. She also refuses to believe the rumors that run rampant on both sides of the border about the colonel's illegal activities. When one is young, Señor Bannock, one sometimes believes with the heart, not the head.

"I remember that it was that way with me when I was a young man. I had fire in my eyes at the sight of a lovely young woman and burning blood that made me yearn to have her and all the other lovelies like her."

Flores smiled ruefully and shook his head in a self-deprecating manner. "But that was long ago and now I only remember the love songs I once sang and do not sing aloud any longer as does my Celia in the dewy mornings and in the late night darkness of her bedroom.

"But you did not come here to listen to me speak of what worries me. You have worries of your own, as you have explained. What is it that you think I can do for you, Señor Bannock?"

"I've been trying to find out what I could from Mexicans on this side of the border about Colonel Mantavo and his plans for more raiding but I've run right up against a stone wall. No one will talk to me. Or they say they know nothing."

"He has intimidated many people, Mantavo has. They are afraid of him so they protect him and profess ignorance of him and his activities."

"That's it. Well, I thought if I could just find somebody who might know what the colonel is up to—and that somebody was willing to pass that information on to me, well, I'd maybe be able to nip in the bud any plans Mantavo has for more raiding and rustling and general hell-raising."

Flores sat back in his chair and cocked an eyebrow at Bannock. "You think I am the man you seek?"

"I do. But I'm willing to admit I may be wrong."

Flores closed his eyes and was silent for a long moment. Then, softly, "I tried to fight Mantavo when I was *alcalde* of Matamoros, as you have heard. In the end, I was unsuccessful.

All my efforts failed. But I wanted—and still want—to see an end once and for all to what Mantavo has been doing. Not only because it makes Mexico look bad in the eyes of you Americanos but also because, to put it quite simply and perhaps a bit foolishly, it is wrong."

Flores opened his eyes and stared at Bannock. "There are not many people in the world today who worry about what is right and what is wrong. They worry about other things. Money—how to get it. Love—where to find it. But I am a child of God and as such I try to do what Holy Mother Church has taught me is the right thing to do. I do not always succeed but I keep trying. That is why I fought Colonel Mantavo when I had power. Now you come here and ask this old man to fight once again."

"I've known old men in my time who were real fine fighters, Señor Flores, because they had a lot of experience. They weren't inclined to go off half-cocked like a lot of hot-blooded younger men would. They were good judges of men and that made them shrewd."

A faint smile appeared on Flores's face. "What you say, señor, it is true. Old men like me have learned a thing or two about human weaknesses and strengths. That knowledge teaches us when to hit and how to hurt and when to bide one's time while waiting for fortune to smile on them."

"I'm willing to pay you one hundred dollars a month for any information you can give me about Colonel Mantavo's future plans and movements."

Flores shook his head.

"One hundred and fifty."

"No, señor, I do not want your money. I will, however, do what you want. It is something I am glad to do. You have given me back something I thought I had lost. Power. The power to do through you what I failed to do on my own. I ask only one thing."

"Whatever it is, I'll give it if it's within my power to do so."

"It must never be known that it is I who am supplying you

with the information that may in time bring Colonel Mantavo to his knees. I'm sure you understand the reason for my request."

"I know what Mantavo would be likely to do to an informer."

"I do not ask for myself but for Celia. If Mantavo were to kill me—what would become of her?"

"I understand."

"Now, tell me this, Señor Bannock. Where can I reach you should I have information of value to you?"

"I'll take a room in the Miller Hotel in Brownsville. You can contact me there. But I'd suggest, since Colonel Mantavo knows me and we're out-and-out enemies, that you not come yourself with the information. If he or one of his men should see us together—well, it wouldn't be good for you, as I'm sure you see."

"A wise suggestion. I have a friend who lives not far from here. His name is Paco Bolivar. He has a young son, Manuel. I will send Manuel to you if I hear of anything you should know."

"Thank you, Señor Flores," Bannock said, rising and holding out his hand.

"Please call me Franco and, if it is all right, I will call you Ben. There is now no need for us to be so formal since we are, as you Americanos say, partners."

The two men shook hands and then Flores escorted Bannock to the front door. He was in the process of ushering his guest outside into the sunshine when a carriage appeared in the distance.

"She comes, my Celia," Flores said, and then in a low tone, almost as if he were talking to himself, "and he is with her."

Bannock recognized Colonel Pedro Mantavo driving the carriage with an attractive woman seated by his side. There was a saddle horse tied behind the vehicle.

"I'd best make myself scarce," he told Flores.

"Inside. Quickly."

Bannock ducked back into the house and closed the front door. He stood there with his back flattened against the wall between the door and an open window through which came the sound of bright girlish laughter and the jingle of harness.

"You are late, Celia," he heard his host say. "I expected you home before this,"

"I met the colonel while I was shopping, Grandfather," Celia answered. "Do not chide me. We stopped and had some *champurrado* together."

"I offered to drive your lovely granddaughter home," Mantavo said. "I was certain you would not mind."

There was a tense moment of silence and then Flores said, "I thank you for escorting Celia home, Colonel. But, in future, we would not think of imposing on you for such courtesies. We know your time is valuable—"

"So is your granddaughter, Don Franco. There are bandits everywhere these days. No trail is safe. So I drove Celia home and now she is here with you, safe and sound."

Bannock heard the note of mockery in Mantavo's voice.

"Thank you very much for your company, Colonel," Celia said. "And for the hot chocolate."

"I told you, my dear," Mantavo said sternly. "You must not be so formal with me. My given name is Pedro."

"Thank you—Pedro," Celia said in a low voice. "I must leave you now."

"Wait!" Flores cried as the door opened. But he was too late. Celia was already inside and standing with an expression of astonishment on her face as she stared at Bannock.

He stepped up to her and closed the door, taking care not to be seen doing so. Then, as Celia opened her mouth to speak, he put a finger to his lips. She remained silent, staring hard at him.

When he was sure that she was not going to create a commotion, he took his finger from his lips and went to the window. He peered cautiously out of it and watched Colonel Mantavo free his horse, which was tied to the rear of the Flores carriage. A moment later, he was in the saddle and riding away without another word to Flores.

The old man waited until his unwelcome guest had disappeared from sight. Only then did he open the door and come inside.

"I did not know you had a guest, Grandfather," Celia declared in a lilting voice, never taking her penetrating eyes from Bannock's face.

"May I present Señor Ben Bannock, Celia."

Celia offered her hand, which Bannock took and kissed.

"Señorita."

Celia Flores was a striking figure of a woman, he decided. A beauty most definitely who would one day soon be even more beautiful. When she matured, the girlishness that now graced her would become more womanly. She would become richer, riper. She would be not merely beautiful then; she would be devastating. Even now she dazzled Bannock. She was almost as tall as he was with straight black hair that framed her face and fell to her shoulders. Her forehead was unlined, her cheeks smooth, her eyes long-lashed. Her lashes seemed to shadow her ebony eyes and make them faintly mysterious. She bore herself with grace, her lithe body making a silent promise any man would long to see fulfilled.

"I am pleased to make your acquaintance, Señor Bannock," she said.

"Señor Bannock was just leaving," Flores interjected.

Bannock, taking the Don's hint, moved toward the door.

"You are a friend of my grandfather I have not met before," Celia said, stopping him in his tracks.

"We only met today, your grandfather and I," he told her.

"We had some business to discuss," Flores explained.

"It must have been secret business, yes, Grandfather? Señor Bannock seemed to be hiding here in the house."

"No, I was—" Bannock shut his mouth since he suddenly found that he could not think of what to say. He felt awed, like a boy in the presence of some superior power. Celia Flores was having an unmistakable effect on him and there was no use trying to deny it.

"When I was a little girl," Celia continued with a smile lighting her eyes, "we would play games. One of us would hide; the others would seek. But we never called it 'business.' "

"I—" Bannock began again and got no farther. What was it about this woman that was making his knees weak and his temperature rise? Her face—her body— He was having trouble breathing.

"I think you were hiding from my escort, Señor Bannock. Are you afraid of Colonel Pedro Mantavo as are, I am told, so many men?"

"Celia," said Flores sharply. "You must not mock my friend."

"Mock? I do not mock him, Grandfather. But he makes me curious. I merely want to find out if I have guessed the truth."

"I wasn't hiding," Bannock protested but was interrupted by Flores.

"Señor Bannock," the Don said, glaring at his granddaughter, "does not get along well with *el Colonel*. In fact, *el Colonel* had raided his ranch in the north and he has come here to try to prevent that from happening to him again or to anyone else."

"Stories, Grandfather," Celia said, her eyes narrowing. "One more of the unproven stories people like to tell about Pedro because he is a brave war hero and they are all jealous of him."

"I am not jealous of Colonel Mantavo," Bannock said, bristling. "What your grandfather has just told you is the truth, Señorita Flores. Mantavo has rustled stock above the border for some time now. He has attacked me and the men who work for me. Or, rather, a gang of bandits led by Diego Anza have done so."

"You will forgive me, señor, if I say I cannot quite bring myself to believe you."

"Celia!" an obviously shocked Flores exclaimed.

"Many people tell stories about what Pedro is supposed to have done—or sent bad men to do for him," an unperturbed Celia continued. "But I have yet to see any proof of such things."

Flores gave Bannock a look of frustrated helplessness.

"I don't know exactly what stories you're talking about Señorita Flores, but I can assure you the story I just told you, if that's what you choose to call it, is completely true."

"So you say." When Bannock's face darkened, Celia hastened to add, "Please, señor, truly I mean no offense. Nor am I calling you a liar. It is just that I grow tired of hearing so many ugly things—so many ugly *unsubstantiated* things—said about a man who is a true courtier. A gentleman and a loyal friend."

Flores sighed. "Celia—"

She hurried on with, "Pedro himself has denied to me that he is involved in any illegal activities. I have told him of the rumors that stain his name. He was indignant. He would, he says, be pleased to meet anyone who is spreading such rumors about him on a field of honor. But no one comes forward to confront him. It is, I think, a sad thing to besmirch a man's good name."

"I agree with you, señorita," Bannock muttered between partially clenched teeth.

Celia's eyes widened. "Then—"

"But I am not telling lies about your—friend." He placed a sly emphasis on his last word, which brought a flush to Celia's face. "You may choose to believe me or not, as you see fit. Suffice it for me to say to you that I do not spread lies to dishonor any man."

"I wish you a pleasant journey back to Brownsville, Ben," Flores said, taking Bannock by the arm and leading him toward the door.

"Wait!"

Both men turned to face Celia. "It is late in the day, Grandfather. The sun is going down. We must not send Señor Bannock away without him having had the opportunity to experience the Flores's famed hospitality. Please unhitch my horse and put him and our carriage away, Grandfather, while I prepare some supper for us. You are hungry, Señor Bannock?"

"Starved." Bannock told himself that he had not really lied. Although he was not exactly starved, he was rather hungry. But he knew that his real reason for responding so swiftly and so positively to Celia Flores's question was the result of his not wanting to leave the lady's presence. Not just yet. "I could eat a horse," he told her, hoping he sounded sincere.

"We have no horse in the larder, señor. But I will see what else I can find." Celia's gaze lingered for a moment on Bannock's face before she turned and left the room, leaving him feeling slightly feverish.

"Sit down, Ben," Flores said. "I will be back soon."

As the old man left the house, Bannock did sit down. But he couldn't sit still. An image of Celia's lovely face and figure flowed in front of his eyes, captivating him and making him restless. He rose and began to pace the room.

He was still pacing when Flores returned some time later. "My granddaughter, forgive her, Ben. She is an outspoken young woman. She must learn to bridle her tongue."

"I find her charming nonetheless."

Flores shot Bannock a speculative glance, which he met with what he hoped was a suitably bland expression.

Later, over supper, Celia turned to him and asked, "What exactly did you come here for, señor?"

"I thought I'd explained that. To try to put a stop to Mantavo's depredations."

"Yes, I understand that. What I do not understand is what all this has to do with my grandfather."

Bannock glanced at Flores, who said, "You know, Celia, I have long opposed what I consider to be evil acts committed by Pedro Mantavo. As *alcalde* of Matamoros, I fought him. To no avail, in the end, sad to say. Now Ben comes here and asks me will I help him fight Mantavo. I say I will and I say so gladly."

Celia put down her fork and stared at her grandfather. "How?"

"Your grandfather is going to keep his eyes and ears open," Bannock told Celia. "He's going to keep me posted about Mantavo's comings and goings so I can maybe get a handle on things and sic the law on the man."

Celia daintily patted her lips with her linen napkin. "I see."

"Colonel Mantavo shames us, Celia," Flores said and took a

sip of his coffee. "He shames Mexico. One day he will bring American troops down upon us. There will be war."

"I do not like this," Celia said, her eyes cast down. "I do not like it at all." She looked up at Bannock. "My grandfather is an old man. He should not be doing this. He is meddling and meddling can be dangerous."

"Then you believe what I've said about Mantavo's rustling and other crimes," Bannock said.

"No, I do not necessarily believe. But I know Pedro is a powerful man in the Army. He is well respected by government officials. If he found out that you"—she glanced at her grandfather—"were spying on him—"

Both men waited for her to finish what she had been saying. When she didn't, when she let her words trail away, Flores asked, "You think he will try to hurt—maybe kill me—my dear?"

Celia bit her lip. "Pedro has a bad temper. Many men do. I think you should not look for trouble, Grandfather."

"I must do what I believe to be right, Celia," Flores said in a low but firm voice.

"Maybe I've stepped in where I don't belong," Bannock said. "Maybe I'd better look elsewhere for help in this Mantavo matter."

"No, Ben," Flores said quickly. "I have said I would do what I can to help you and I will. I am a man of my word. But that is not the only reason I am willing to help you. There are at least two others. One is that I believe evil must be sought out and destroyed. And Mantavo is evil incarnate, in my opinion.

"The second reason is that I have fought him in the past and lost. Now you give me this chance to fight him again. You give an old man a second chance to fight his enemy and, if the good God will smile on me, perhaps a chance to finally win the fight."

Celia slammed her small fists down on the table, rattling the china and causing the cutlery to clatter. "Grandfather, this is foolishness. You are no longer a young man, as you say yourself. It is young men who rush off to fight in battles. Old men do not do such things. Old men have more sense."

Flores smiled. "Not all old men are wise, my dear. You are looking at one who is a young man at heart and afflicted with all the vices of young men—hotheadedness, pride and an overeagerness to conquer those who stain the world with their sins."

"Gentlemen, please excuse me." Celia threw down her napkin and stood up so quickly she almost overturned her chair. She fled from the room, her long black skirt swirling about her legs.

Bannock and Flores exchanged glances.

Flores shrugged.

"She loves you," Bannock said. "She doesn't want me around because she figures I might be the means of bringing you harm."

"It is that, *sí*. But it is also more. She does not want to believe the truth about her Colonel Mantavo."

Her Colonel Mantavo.

Why, Bannock wondered, did those words make him uncomfortable? No, more than merely uncomfortable. Why did they make him faintly angry as well? Was he—could it be that he was jealous of Mantavo's relationship with Celia Flores?

"There is another thing to be gained if I can help you defeat Mantavo," Flores said thoughtfully.

"What is that?"

"It will end his courting of my granddaughter. I have been wishing for that to happen for a long time. But until today I could see no way to accomplish it. She did not listen to me when I asked her to stay away from him. If I had spoken to Mantavo himself he would have laughed in my face. But now—now that goal I have been seeking may be within my reach."

"There's an old American saying, Franco. 'Don't count your chickens before they're hatched.' "

"A very good saying it is. I shall keep it in mind."

Bannock silently promised himself that he would do the same in the days ahead as he sought for a way to triumph over Mantavo and his brush-riders. But he was keenly aware that his determination to defeat the colonel once and for all was fueled now by something more than just the desire to protect his stock and ranch from the man's raiders. Now there was an additional benefit to be gained from such a defeat. Flores had defined it clearly. Such a defeat would mean not only the end of Mantavo's illegal activities; it would also mean—at least Bannock sincerely hoped it would mean—the end of the developing relationship between Pedro Mantavo and Celia Flores.

"It is time for me to go, Franco," he told his host.

Both men rose and Flores accompanied Bannock as he made his way outside. The older man stood by as Bannock stepped into the saddle and then said, "I will be in touch with you, Ben. Soon, I hope. I will visit my many friends in this area and along the border. If I hear of anything that might be of interest to you I will send Manuel Bolivar to you with the news."

"I'll be looking forward to hearing from you, Franco."

"Good-bye, my friend."

It was dark when Bannock checked into the Miller Hotel in Brownsville. Once in his room, he lay down on the bed, his hands clasped behind his head, and stared at the ceiling.

But it was not the ceiling he saw. It was the lovely face and as lovely figure of Celia Flores. She of the dark mysterious eyes and full inviting lips. She who had somehow, Bannock knew not how, shattered all the defenses that he had so carefully constructed over the years. Defenses which had kept him safe from the seductive siren song of love between a man and a woman— the defenses that had kept him safe from the risk of loving, and possibly losing, another woman as he had lost, years ago, his beloved wife, Nora.

Celia shared the room with him as the minutes passed and later she shared his dreams when he was finally able to sleep. During the next two seemingly endless days a restless Bannock prowled the streets and stores and saloons of Brownsville. He talked to everyone who would listen to him, both Americans and Mexicans. He talked to them of cattle rustling. He mentioned the names of Diego Anza and Pedro Mantavo. He learned nothing.

But he saw the fear in the faces of many of the Mexicans when he mentioned the pair of names. And he heard Americans denounce the rustling and the rustlers in violent and, occasionally, distinctly racist terms, calling them "dirty greasers" and worse. Bannock heard the drums of a race war beating and the bugles of bigotry blowing.

Every woman he saw in the streets and stores during those two days reminded him of Celia Flores. The curve of this one's cheek, the thrust of that one's pert breasts. But the real Celia eluded him. He had to be content with ghosts and ghosts of ghosts—all resembling Celia but none of them really her—an experience he found subtly tormenting.

There was one man he met in the Lone Star Saloon on the afternoon of his second day in town, a Mexican, who stood his ground instead of sidling away when Bannock mentioned the infamous colonel.

That man said that he would, had he at some time in the future the nerve and the opportunity, do terrible things to certain private parts of the bodies of four men who he knew rode for Mantavo, one of them scar-faced. The stranger told Bannock, with a blend of fire and ice in his eyes, that they'd attacked his sister as they passed the man's home that morning while riding toward the Valley of the Vultures.

The four had ravished his sister after tieing the man to a tree where he could do nothing but listen helplessly to his sister's anguished screams.

The Valley of the Vultures, Bannock knew, lay north of the border and due east of Brownsville. On an impulse, he went to the livery and saddled his bay. Then he rode out of town, heading east.

When he reached the top of a hill overlooking the Valley of the Vultures, he found the place to be aptly named. Vultures nested on the craggy hills surrounding the valley. They filled the sky like vermin, swooping and banking on the updrafts of air from the valley far below them.

Bannock sat his saddle on the crest of one of the rugged hills, his hands wrapped around his saddle horn, and gazed out over the vast expanse of the valley. Mist drifted in places within it and crowned some of the hills' sharp crags. He could not see the far side of the valley in the distance but he heard what he thought at first was thunder rumbling faintly in that direction.

No, not thunder. The rumbling was too sharp and too percussive to be thunder. What he was hearing, Bannock realized, was gunfire.

He slammed his spurs into his horse's flanks and went galloping down the steeply sloping hill and across the valley floor as he headed toward the deadly sound in the distance.

EIGHT

THE MIST swirled about him as he rode, urging his horse with his spurs and knee pressure to give him every bit of speed the animal could muster. Dampness coated his face and hands with a slick sheen as he neared the source of the sound of the gunfire that was like some deadly and erratic drumbeat up ahead of him.

Then, as he burst into another world, one that was almost totally mistless, he saw a horse herd ahead of him and nearly a dozen men firing at one another. He was able to see that one side was composed of four men—Diego Anza and three other bandits—and that the other consisted of the herd's defenders.

Taking in the lay of the land and the position of the horse herd relative to the Mexicans, it took him only seconds to plan a strategy. He slammed his spurs into his bay's flanks and headed for the herd, removing his coiled rope from his saddle horn as he went.

"It's *him!*" he heard Anza shout in outraged Spanish. And then, *"Kill* him!"

When a round whined past his left ear, he dropped down low, hugging his horse's neck while giving it free rein. As he rode up on the right flank of the herd, he switched his rope from his right to his left hand. He flailed at the horses that were so close to him he could feel the heat given off by their bodies.

His rope slashed a dapple, which screamed and threw itself to one side, colliding with the horse next to it, which promptly retaliated for the blow by snapping at the dapple and drawing blood from its neck. He continued swinging his rope, hitting first one horse and then another one. His rope landed on a buckskin's snout with a crackling sound. The buckskin turned and reared, trying to escape the hail of blows. Bannock hit it again.

The buckskin, the dapple and several other targets of Bannock's rope lunged into the main body of the herd to escape the punishing blows. In doing so, they started the stampede Bannock had been trying to initiate. The herd bolted, the manes of the fleeing animals flying out behind them as they raced away from their tormentor, their great eyes rolling in fear, their hooves tearing up the ground.

Bannock went after them. Using his reins and his knees, he moved his bay to the right, then to the left, back to the right again, to keep the herd in line. His loop landed on the rump of a horse that was about to bolt to the right away from the main herd. The blow brought the animal back into line.

Bannock heard one of the Mexicans scream as the horse herd bore down on them. Minutes later, he slowed his bay. Then he turned it into some trees where he sat his saddle watching and waiting to see the outcome of his retaliatory maneuver.

"You wanted our horses," he heard one of the herd's defenders shout with glee in his voice. "Well, you're gonna get 'em, you thieving bastards!"

Bannock's lips parted slightly in a sardonic grin as he watched the fleeing Mexicans. Two had managed to board their mounts —one of them was Anza. The other two were scrambling desperately to escape the oncoming horses. One shinnied up a cottonwood. The other man fleeing on foot was not so fortunate. He went down under the hooves of the relentlessly advancing herd of horses. He screamed abortively an instant before the life was crushed from him.

Bannock stood up in his stirrups and watched the horses race on. Beyond them he saw no sign of Anza or the man riding with him. His eyes drifted to the man clinging to an upper branch of the cottonwood. He drew his gun and rode over to the tree.

"Get down," he ordered the Mexican, whose gun, he had noticed, was gone.

"Don't shoot!" the man responded as he gingerly began to ease down the trunk of the tree. "I'm not armed."

"*Down!*" was Bannock's only response.

Once the Mexican's feet touched the ground, Bannock leveled his revolver at the man, whose hands promptly shot up into the air.

"Where were you going to hit next?" Bannock asked him as several of the herd's defenders came running up to join him.

"Shoot him!" one of the men yelled before the Mexican could answer Bannock's question.

"Get out of the way!" another man ordered, trying to elbow Bannock aside as he took aim at the terrified Mexican with his sidearm.

Bannock slammed the barrel of his revolver down on the man's wrist, snapping it and knocking the gun from his hand.

"*Owwww!*" the man cried, hopping about and trying to cradle his helplessly dangling hand with his other hand.

"Why, you sonofabitch!" another man bellowed. "I thought you was on *our* side!"

"I'm on my side," Bannock said quietly. "Any man who makes a move I don't like, and that means any move at all, I'll drill him."

The men froze. They exchanged tense glances but no words.

"That's it," Bannock said calmly. "Now you'll all stay the way you are or I'll let light through you." He turned his attention once again to his prisoner, who was visibly trembling as he stood with his back pressed against the cottonwood's trunk. "I asked you a question. I'm not going to wait much longer for an answer."

"I do not know the answer, señor, I truly do not. Diego, he decides where we will go and when. He does not tell us in advance. Today we come here. Tomorrow—who knows?"

"I think you know."

"No, señor, I know nothing. It is Diego Anza who knows."

"Where will I find Anza and the man who got away with him? You got a camp around here, have you?"

"No, señor, no camp. We planned to go back to Mexico with the horses we take but—you came. Now—I do not know what Diego will do next or where he will go."

Bannock put a bullet into the cottonwood's trunk only an inch from the right side of the Mexican's head.

The man screamed and started to make a run for it. Bannock's next round bit into the ground in front of the man's flying feet. It brought him to an abrupt halt.

"Turn around."

The Mexican slowly turned around.

"I've got a bullet in this gun that says you're lying to me."

"No, no, señor, I do not lie! Please, I can tell you nothing."

Bannock's next shot ripped into the fleshy part of the Mexican's left forearm.

The man screamed and seized his arm from which blood was flowing in a bright red stream.

Bannock, watching the man with one eye and the horse herd defenders with the other, calculated the odds that the Mexican was telling the truth. He decided the man really didn't know Anza's next move. He would have told me by now, he thought, rather than risk me wounding his other arm or, maybe, one of his legs. He watched the Mexican, who was sobbing and shaking his head as if to deny the reality of his own leaking blood.

Then, "He's yours if you want him," he said to the tense defenders of the horse herd.

He was about to turn his horse and ride out after Anza and his companion when one of the men said, "Mister, we don't know where you came from but we sure as hell are happy you came!"

"Glad I could be of some help to you boys."

"Help? Mister, you weren't just help. You saved the day for us. Those horse thieves had us pinned down real good until you rode in. They winged Virge here and nearly stopped my clock at one point. They probably would have if you hadn't of shown up."

"Be seeing you." Bannock moved out.

When he heard screaming behind him followed by malicious laughter, he looked back over his shoulder. The men whose horse herd had been attacked were tieing a noose around the neck of the Mexican Bannock had left behind.

One of the men tossed the loose end of the rope over the limb of a tree and pulled it taut. Several other men got a grip on the rope and with a shouted, "Heave *ho!*" they pulled on it, their backs bent with the effort. As they moved away from the tree, the Mexican, his hands clawing at the tightening noose around his neck, was hauled off the ground and up into the air where he swung back and forth while simultaneously turning in a slow circle.

He no longer screamed. He could no longer make the slightest sound, let alone a scream. He struggled frantically, his face contorted into a ghastly mask, his skin darkening, turning purple, his tongue pushing its way out from between his twisted lips as if in some childish display of petulance directed at his captors.

Suddenly, his hands flew away from the rope that was slowly squeezing the life out of him. They shot convulsively outward, hung suspended at right angles to his body for a moment and then fell to slap lifelessly against his thighs. The man swung and slowly spun at the end of the rope, his head at a forty-five-degree angle to his body, his eyes bulging and blood dripping onto his shirt from the tongue he had bitten almost in half during his brief agony.

Bannock turned and rode on.

He searched the ground for sign as he rode and soon found the hot trail left by Anza and the man who was still riding with him. Their horses' hooves had dug deeply into the ground and their imprints were far apart, both signs of hard and fast flight.

Twenty minutes later, he spotted his quarry directly ahead of him as they crossed a savannah where the grasses growing on it were tall enough to brush their boots. He increased his pace, intending to narrow the distance between himself and the two Mexicans enough to bring them within range of his revolver.

They must have heard him. Or sensed his presence behind them. Both men turned at the same time. Seeing their pursuer, they lashed their mounts with their reins and went galloping through the tall grass, heading due south.

Bannock vowed they would not escape from him. He would follow them all the way to South America if necessary. He would catch up to them, he promised himself. And when he did he wouldn't stop to ask questions this time. He intended to shoot both men—and shoot to kill them as he would shoot a cougar or a coyote that was threatening his cattle.

He drew his six-gun. Dropping his reins, he thumbed cartridges out of his belt and reloaded the weapon. Then, picking up his reins, he did as his quarry was doing. He lashed his horse's withers. The wind ripped past his face as the bay gave him a new burst of speed.

Up ahead, the Rio Bravo suddenly came into view at the level of the horizon. Anza and his companion were heading straight for it. In what seemed like almost no time at all, they had reached the shallow river and gone splashing across it into Mexico. They had no sooner done so than several mounted soldiers appeared off to their left.

Bannock had almost reached the river when Anza joined the soldiers and, turning in his saddle, pointed at Bannock and spoke in swift Spanish to the armed men. With barely a moment's hesitation, the soldiers drew their guns and placed themselves between the two bandits and the southern bank of the river. As Bannock approached them, they silently took aim at him, all of them.

He drew rein, bringing his bay to a skidding halt about twenty yards from the river.

"Señor," one of the soldiers called out to him. "If you cross the Rio Bravo to commit a crime against Mexican citizens, we will have to shoot you."

"In the heart," added the mounted man next to the soldier who had just spoken. He grinned, baring blunt yellow teeth.

Cursing softly under his breath, Bannock leathered his gun.

"You are a wise man, señor," said the now smirking soldier who had first spoken.

"You are a man who does not want to die," observed the soldier with the yellow teeth.

Then all of them turned their horses and rode away from the river. They surrounded Anza and the man with him and escorted them both away from the river and the man who had vowed to kill them.

Bannock watched them go, fury born of frustration raging within him. Not now, he thought. Not today. But someday. Someday soon we will meet again, Anza, and when we do I will kill you. Or you will kill me. We have, you and I, a blood feud between us. It must be satisfied. The death of one of us will do that.

He turned his horse and rode away from the river, thinking: Soon, Anza, soon.

The next day Bannock rode out to the Flores rancho. He chided himself as he made the journey for watching his shadow on the ground—the tilt, just so, of his hat; the straightness of his spine. You've not been a shadow rider since you were a boy, he thought. Then you were always checking your appearance as you rode country lanes on your way to a harvest-home dance or to court some pretty girl who would, if you were the least bit lucky, walk out with you under the summer stars and maybe, if you were the luckiest of men . . .

And now?

The name came to him and rang in his ears, a sweet soft bell: Celia Flores.

An image of her loveliness stirred his heart and lifted his spirits. He had told himself that morning that it was time he went to call on Franco Flores. Time to find out what, if anything, Franco had found out about Colonel Mantavo's plans. But as he applied some of the Number Six Cologne he had bought from a Brownsville druggist to his face and chest he knew he wanted to see Celia as much, if not more, than he did the old man.

"The ladies do seem to like it," the druggist had told him. "In fact, many do indeed dote on it, or so I am told by the young gay blades about town. The formula contains twenty-seven—I do not exaggerate, sir—natural ingredients among which are numbered musk, orange blossom, bergamot and lemon. Number Six Cologne, sir, was much favored by the father of our country, Mr. George Washington. He liked it so much that he sent two bottles of the concoction to his old ally Lafayette to enjoy."

"How much?" Bannock asked, opening the box and then the bottle it contained and sniffing.

"Three ounces are one dollar and five cents, sir. It comes also in eight- and sixteen-ounce sizes."

Bannock bought an eight-ounce bottle and later as he was applying it he saw in the mirror not himself but the enticingly smiling face of Celia Flores.

And now, as he rode at a faster pace than he knew to be necessary, it was she who beckoned him on with whispered promises that heated his blood and fed his dreams.

When he arrived at the rancho, he saw no signs of life and, for a brief moment, his heart sank. Was no one home? Was *she* not at home? He dismounted and wrapped his reins around the hitch rail in front of the house. He knocked on the door and stood waiting in the sun, listening eagerly for any sound from inside the house.

He heard footsteps beyond the door. Light; not those of a man. He squared his shoulders and fixed a smile on his face.

"Good day, Señor Bannock," Celia Flores said after recovering from her surprise at seeing Bannock on her doorstep.

"Señorita Flores," he said, unable to take his eyes from her face. "I thought it might be a good idea to come out here and have a talk with your grandfather about—the matter that concerns both of us."

"Come in, please."

Once inside the house, Celia took a seat where the light of the sun streaming through the ornate lace curtains covering the window haloed her head and made the saffron gown she wore seem to glow.

"My grandfather is not at home, Señor Bannock."

The news did not disturb or annoy Bannock. "I hope you and I are going to be friends. To that end, I wonder if it wouldn't be a good idea for you to call me Ben."

Celia studied him for a moment and then, "I shall—if you'll call me Celia."

"It would be a pleasure."

She seemed to be waiting for him to go on. But, suddenly, he could think of nothing to say. His mind whirled. His cheeks reddened in embarrassment. He opened his mouth to speak. No words came.

Celia came to his rescue with, "Do you have many cattle on your ranch, señor—Ben?"

He managed a nod. And then, miraculously, words.

"Close to three thousand head. This spring's increase was a good one—truly bountiful. The cows that bear my Double B brand could cover a good third of Texas if we spread them out a bit."

"You have many men who help you work your cattle?"

"Yes, a goodly number."

"Is something wrong?" Celia asked, leaning forward slightly in her chair when she saw Bannock's face darken. "Did I say something wrong?"

He looked up at her. "No, you didn't. It's just that I was remembering . . ."

"Remembering?"

"I had a foreman—he happened to also be a very good friend of mine. His name was Wes Holbrook. He was killed—shot to death—in a run-in me and my men had with some of Colonel Mantavo's bravos. Your question—it made me think of him."

It was Celia's turn to show distress. Her hands, which had been resting quietly in her lap, gripped the arms of her chair.

"Colonel Mantavo is like a ghost that haunts us—our every conversation."

"I'm sorry. I didn't mean to bring his name up. It's just that—"

Celia waved Bannock's words away. "I am sorry to hear that you lost a good friend."

"My ranch," Bannock said, trying to shift the emphasis of the conversation to a safer subject, "is, I readily confess, my pride and joy. I built it up from scratch. I bought my first twenty acres when I had more holes than soles on the bottoms of my boots. Not to mention a whole lot of patches on my pants. I'd saved and scraped together the money for a long time to buy those first twenty acres. Once I'd done so, it didn't seem to matter one whit to me that I'd been eating one meal a day for so long I'd gotten skinny enough to take a bath in a rifle barrel."

Celia matched Bannock's smile, encouraging him to go on.

"It was a small start I made but it was a start and that's what was important. I worked that little spread of mine from can-see to can't-see and I never complained. Fact was, I didn't feel like I had anything to complain about. I had my land. I had a few cows that I'd taken in place of wages from the last ranch I worked before I went out on my own. I was young and strong—I'd just turned nineteen. So what I reckon I'm saying is it was a hard life but a real good one. It was one I tell you I truly prized."

When Bannock paused for a moment, fondly remembering his early days as a cattle rancher, Celia spoke. "You lived alone on your ranch?"

"I did, yes."

She arched an eyebrow. "You had no woman with whom to share your home or your life?"

Bannock looked down at the floor for a moment. Then, meeting Celia's probing gaze, he said, "There was a woman once. Her name was Nora."

As he stared at Celia sitting in the golden beams of light streaming through the window, Bannock suddenly saw, not Celia, but his beloved Nora. He was surprised to realize that the two women shared certain characteristics he had failed to notice before. Celia had Nora's aquiline nose. Like Celia's, Nora's ears had been pierced and usually displayed small golden earrings. Both women had slender hands with long tapering fingers. Celia shared with Nora the habit of opening her lips slightly as she organized her thoughts before speaking.

Was it these shared characteristics then that formed the basis of his strong attraction to Celia Flores, he wondered. He rejected the idea. Celia was a woman in her own right as was Nora. Though the two might share certain characteristics, they were, in most ways, as different as night and day. Nora's beauty was of the sun and the day—bright and shining. Celia, on the other hand, struck Bannock as a daughter of the night. She shared its dark beauty. Then, too, there was the matter of nationality. Celia was Mexican. Nora had been an American of Scotch/Irish descent. Where Nora had tended to be placid, Celia was mercurial in the way she spoke and moved.

"You were in love with her—this Nora?" Celia asked softly, never taking her eyes from Bannock's solemn face.

"In love with her? I was. She was my sunrise and the stars in my night's sky. Nora was everything to me. She—I can't tell you how much I loved that woman. When we married, I was the happiest man on the face of this old earth."

"She is not with you now?"

Bannock dropped his gaze. He shook his head. "She died."

Celia drew back as if she had been threatened. Then, softly, "Ben, I'm sorry."

He nodded wordlessly.

"You never had any children, you and Nora?"

"She was pregnant when she died of pleurisy." Bannock rose and went to the window where he stood staring out in silence.

Celia also remained silent, staring at his broad back.

"When Nora died, I didn't think I could go on. I did nothing for a long time. My ranch—I let it run down. A man has to keep on top of things with a ranch like mine else things go to rack and ruin so fast it would make your head swim. Fences fall. Stock sickens and sometimes dies. Buildings fall into disrepair.

"I knew that—saw it happening all around me. But, to tell the truth, I didn't give a damn. Excuse me, Celia. But it's the truth. That's the way I felt at the time. I just did not care whether school kept or not."

"It must have been a terrible time for you."

Bannock clasped his hands behind his back. "It *was* terrible. I used to go out to the spot where I buried Nora. There was a willow tree that grew there and I used to sit under it next to her grave and curse God and cry. Neither the cursing nor the crying did one bit of good for me or for Nora. She was gone and I was alone again and that, unhappily, was that.

"Things went on like that for nearly a year. Then one day I was out at Nora's grave and talking to her the way I used to do and all at once I heard her voice. I can still hear her to this very day. She told me I must stop what I was doing—the way I was behaving. She reminded me of all the plans we had made together. She told me I must keep on living. I must, she said, do all the things we had planned to do together. I must not give in, she told me, to grief. I must not let it be my master as it had been for so long.

"I sat there stunned. Nora said she would be watching me. She did not want to be forced to believe, she told me, that she had married someone who was unable to bear the admittedly awful burden the good Lord had placed on his shoulders. In the end—the last thing she said to me was 'Ben, be happy. Be happy for both of us.' "

Bannock turned from the window to face Celia. "I didn't mean to talk so much about myself. What I'd really like is to have you tell me about yourself."

Celia made a move. Shrugged. "There's really nothing to tell. I'm not an important person. Nothing very exciting has ever happened to me."

"I understand you were born in Mexico," Bannock prompted.

"*Sí.* Near Matamoros. My parents were farmers. They are both gone now as is your Nora." Celia quickly hurried on as if she had said something indiscreet. "I had an ordinary girlhood. There was school during the week and church on Sundays. When I grew up, there were *caballeros* who came calling."

"I'm sure there were. Did you ever find yourself in love with any of them?"

Celia laughed, a pleasant, almost musical sound. "Of course. I fell in love with all of them! One right after the other!"

"I'll bet you broke all their hearts."

Coquettishly: "I would never do such a thing. You can ask"— Celia hesitated a moment and then—"Colonel Mantavo. I have not broken his heart."

Bannock regretted and faintly resented the turn the conversation had suddenly taken but he did not let his feelings show. Nor did he follow up on Celia's remark. Instead, he said, "I can readily understand why the boys flocked to you when you were a girl and why men would be attracted to the woman you have become. If you will permit me to say so, you are very lovely, Celia."

"You flatter me."

"I tell the truth."

"Would you like some coffee, Ben? I have some little cakes that I made yesterday."

"Coffee would be fine."

As Celia rose and was passing him as he continued to stand by the window, he resisted the impulse to reach out and take her in his arms. A faint scent of perfume wafted from her as she went past him on her way out of the room.

When she returned she was carrying a silver tray on which rested a coffeepot and china cups. She sat down and proceeded to fill a cup which she handed to Bannock. Then she poured a cup of coffee for herself.

Bannock took a seat beside her on an overstuffed sofa. They were talking of the weather and other things of no consequence when Bannock heard the sound of a carriage and harness jingling outside.

"My grandfather returns," Celia said.

A moment later the door opened and Franco Flores strode into the room.

"Ah, Ben Bannock, you have come back to my home. It is good to see you again."

Bannock put down his cup, rose and shook hands with Flores. "I thought I'd check with you to see what, if anything, you have heard about our mutual friend." He avoided looking at Celia when he spoke the last euphemistic phrase. "And to report to you an encounter I had with some of Mantavo's black-hearted minions."

"Coffee, Grandfather?" When her grandfather nodded, Celia poured a cup and handed it to the old man.

"I have no news to give you, Ben," Flores announced. "I have spoken to many people in this area but they know nothing. They *say* they know nothing. Which does not necessarily mean that they do indeed know nothing. It is the way of things where the colonel is concerned. He is a powerful man and can be a cruel one. People have learned to fear him and those he employs to do his dirty work." Flores sipped from his cup. "You say you had an encounter with him?"

"No, not with him. With Diego Anza and three other bandits. They were raiding a horse herd that was being grazed in the Valley of the Vultures."

"You knew they would do this?"

"No. I'd done some inquiring of various people but got no farther really than you did, Franco. Then I happened to run into a fellow . . ."

Flores listened intently as Bannock related his tale of meeting the Mexican whose sister had suffered at the hands of Mantavo and his men and his subsequent journey to the Valley of the Vultures in search of those same men.

"It is like trying to trap the wind," Flores said when Bannock had finished his account of the incident. "Impossible."

"I won't accept that," Bannock stated bluntly. "They are just men like us. They have their strengths but they also have their weaknesses. One day we will win out over them."

"You talk like this is a war you are fighting," Celia said, anger lurking in her voice.

"It is a war," Bannock insisted.

"Men love war," Celia declared, turning away from him. "Women love peace. It is no wonder then that we can seldom agree on things such as this."

"Peace has many virtues, my dear," Flores said gently. "But there are times when war must be waged if for no other reason than to stamp out evil."

Celia turned around to face the two men. "Who decides what is evil? One side says it is the other side that is evil. The other side says no, it is those men over there who are evil. It is a boy's game played by grown men who should know better. It would be silly if it were not so dangerous."

"I've got no problem identifying evil when I meet up with it," Bannock said. "What Mantavo and his men are doing is evil if evil means wrong."

"What Mantavo and his men are doing," Celia quoted, her eyes flashing. "You do not know that Pedro Mantavo steals American cattle. You have no proof. You have not seen him do this thing that you say he does, have you?"

Bannock had to admit she was right. "But there's no doubt in my mind that he's behind it. None whatsoever."

Celia tossed her head, a gesture of disdain bordering on contempt. "It must be nice to be so sure of things in one's life. Nice to know that all is either black or white, good or bad. Nice to know that there are no grays in one's life to confuse one. Or make one stop to think."

Bannock almost flinched under her verbal assault. He watched her hurry out of the room.

When the door slammed behind her, he glanced at Flores, who sighed and said, "The young are passionate. Sometimes their passion leads them astray. But I would not have it any other way. Much good comes from the passion of the young when it is wedded to truth and justice. Unfortunately, harm sometimes comes from passion that is blinded by love."

Bannock's eyes narrowed. "Are you saying, Franco, that Celia is in love with Pedro Mantavo?"

"It may be so. I do not really know. I know only that she and that man, they sometimes look at one another with eyes of longing and desire. But longing and desire are not always the same thing as love."

"I think I'll go outside and tell her I'm sorry I upset her, if that's all right with you."

"Go, Ben. And remember. Passion in the young is like a fire. No fire burns forever."

"If you hear anything—"

"I will send word to you."

Bannock left the room and hurried outside to find Celia standing with her arms folded across her chest and gazing out into the empty distance. He stepped up behind her and said, "I'd like to come back tomorrow and visit you again."

Celia said nothing.

"I'll rent a rig. We could take a drive out into the countryside."

He put his hands on her shoulders and turned her toward him. "Maybe by tomorrow you won't be mad at me anymore."

Her eyes flashed momentarily and then softened. Her lips parted in a slight smile. "One can be mad only at someone one cares about in some way. Otherwise, without the caring, there is no reason to get mad. One would simply dismiss the other person in that case—if one cared nothing for him."

Bannock drew Celia close to him. He bent his head and their lips met and held.

When they parted, Celia looked up at him. "I will make some things for us to eat when you come back tomorrow. We will have a *merienda*—a picnic."

"That sounds just fine. Wonderful, in fact. I'll be here tomorrow at—will noon be all right?"

"Noon will be fine. I will be ready."

Bannock kissed Celia again and then went to his horse.

He was about to step into the saddle when Celia said, "Ben."

When she had his attention, she said, "There is in my language a saying that goes like this: *'Quien llama el toro aguanta la cornada.'* "

"My Spanish is not that good—"

"It means 'He who calls the bull must endure the horn wound.' "

Bannock knew what she meant. He swung into the saddle, touched the brim of his hat to Celia and rode out thinking about Colonel Pedro Mantavo—the man Celia had just referred to so ominously.

NINE

BEFORE LEAVING Brownsville the next morning, Bannock stopped at the telegraph office to see if he had received a reply to the message he had sent the night before to his new ranch foreman.

"This came for you early this morning," the telegraph operator told him as he handed over a message from Viviano Colorado.

Bannock read it quickly and was relieved to learn that there had been no trouble at the ranch since he left. But he was bitterly disappointed also to learn that he had received replies to the telegraph messages he had sent to state and federal elected officials before leaving and all of them had said there was no help they could offer at this time. The governor of Texas was, according to Viviano, "taking the matter under advisement." Legislators in Congress did not want to "exacerbate present tensions between Mexico and the United States of America." But they promised to "appoint a committee to study the matter."

He left the office and drove out of town in the rig he had rented.

When he had arrived at his destination, he parked the rig in front of the house and knocked on the door.

Franco Flores answered the door and ushered Bannock into

the house. "Celia is almost ready," the old man announced. "But you had better sit down, Ben. 'Almost ready' to women usually means a long wait. I swear they do it on purpose to make us men nervous. Would you like some brandy?"

"No, thank you," Bannock said as he sat down.

"Coffee?"

Bannock shook his head. He wanted neither brandy nor coffee—only Celia.

When she came gliding into the room some ten minutes later, she looked radiant. Her eyes glowed. So did her smooth skin. Her hair, which she had bound into a pony tail with a scarlet ribbon, shone in the sunlight streaming through the windows. She wore a full-skirted white cotton dress, the hem of which was bedecked with miniature scarlet ribbons to match the larger one holding her hair in place. She carried a wide-brimmed straw hat with a white ribbon encircling its crown.

"Oh," she declared, stopping in her tracks. "I almost forgot." She hurried out of the room. When she returned she was carrying a large wicker picnic hamper which she handed to Bannock.

"Before you go, Ben," her grandfather said, "I should tell you that I have still learned nothing that would help you in your efforts to stop Mantavo."

Bannock found himself experiencing conflicting feelings as a result of Flores's statement. On the one hand, he was sorry to hear that there was no progress from Flores's end of the issue. On the other, he was relieved that Flores had nothing to tell him which would interfere in any way with the day and the picnic he and Celia had planned.

"I thank you for keeping your ear to the ground, Franco," he said.

Then he and Celia left the house and he helped her into the carriage he had rented. She took the hamper from him and he climbed into the driver's seat, slapped the rump of the horse with the reins and they were off.

"I know of a place," Celia said. "There is a lake, a small one, and many trees. In the distance, there are hills. No one lives there. It is a place made for picnics. Shall I show you the way?"

"By all means."

They arrived at the place Celia had described in less than an hour and Bannock found it to be everything she said it was. Lovely, quiet and uninhabited except for a roadrunner that fled at their approach, leaving the spot to them.

Celia spread a checkered cloth she had packed in her hamper on the ground and then set out the food she had prepared.

They ate, sitting side by side, their shoulders occasionally touching, as fat white clouds drifted between the crags of the distant hills and a bird sang somewhere out of sight.

"I used to come here when I was a girl," Celia said as she ate some cold roast beef she had placed on a slice of homemade bread spread with butter. "I used to pretend that this was my secret kingdom and I was its queen. I had, when I was young, a head full of fancies."

"Everybody needs a place to call his very own kingdom," Bannock said, biting into a piece of goat cheese and savoring its zesty flavor. "Even if it's only a cave in a hill somewhere."

Celia rose and hurried down to the edge of the lake where she had placed a crock of milk in the water to keep it cool. She brought it back and filled a cup, which she handed to Bannock.

He took the cup from her and placed it on the ground. Impulsively, he reached out, took Celia in his arms and kissed her passionately.

At first, she did not respond. Then, as their lips remained locked together, her arms went around him and she began to return his kiss.

"Celia, I have to tell you," he said a breathless moment later. "I've never felt like this—the way I do right now—with any other woman before except the one I married."

"Nora."

"Yes, Nora. It was as if I were not really alive inside anymore after I lost her. Or as if a part of me had died. But all that changed when I met you. Right from the start it was like you put a match to my heart and set it on fire. I thought the things I felt in your presence would never be mine to feel anymore. But you —somehow you made me—awaken. Awaken to a part of me that had lain buried for all the years since Nora—went."

Celia's hands rose. She cupped Bannock's face between her palms, gently kissed his lips and then released him.

"Once things settle down some," he began, "once Mantavo's out of the picture and the raiding's finally over and done with—"

"I don't want to talk about Pedro Mantavo."

Bannock was glad to hear it while simultaneously regretting the fact that he had brought the man's name into the conversation. But now that he had, he made up his mind to ask Celia the question that had been on his mind and which was bothering him more and more each day.

"Celia, are you in love with Mantavo?"

She looked away, off toward the cloud-capped hills. "He has asked me to marry him."

Celia's announcement chilled Bannock. "That's not an answer to the question I asked you."

She looked back at him. "Am I in love with Pedro? I don't know. That is the truth, Ben. I truly do not know. I do know I like him. But love him?

"Mexican marriages are not always made because two people love each other. Many things enter into the making of marriages among my people. Power, for one. Money, for another. A woman marries a man because he is the *alcalde* of a large town and therefore powerful. A man marries a woman because her family owns a vast Spanish land grant so his sons will be able to live lives of privilege. It has been and still is this way among my people."

"What did you tell him when he asked you to marry him?"

"I did not give him an answer."

"But you will?"

"I suppose so."

"When and what will it be?"

"Ben, you ask so many questions—too many."

Bannock decided he had better back off. His eagerness to hear her say that Pedro Mantavo was out of the romantic running was, he realized, causing him to put too much pressure on her. And, he also decided, he was being presumptuous in doing so. Whether she loved or would marry Mantavo was not the question. The real question was whether he could make Celia Flores fall in love with him and, in time, marry him.

He lay down on the ground on his back and stared up at the drifting clouds which occasionally blinded the sun. "It's nice being here with you, just the two of us."

She lay down beside him, one hand supporting her head, and stared down at him. "We are very different, you and I. You are an American, for example, and I am Mexican. How is it that we are here together today and not still strangers?"

"A card sharp would probably call it the luck of the draw," he answered, reaching up and running a finger down her nose. "A priest would call it the grace of God. I call it destiny."

She made a face. "Such a strong word, destiny."

"Then tell me. How do you explain it?"

"Our being together here today? I do not explain it. I cannot. I just enjoy it and pretend that it will never end."

"I wish it wouldn't. I wish we could be together like this forever. Every day that is left of our lives and every minute of those days."

"That is neither possible nor practical."

"We could make it possible. Maybe even practical. We could—"

"You didn't drink your milk."

Bannock glanced at the cup full of milk he had placed on the ground nearby. He picked it up and drained it.

Then, at Celia's suggestion, they rose and began to circle the lake. Halfway around it, Bannock took her hand. He led her into the shadows shed by a stand of mesquite trees and there he kissed her again. As his hands began to fumble with the bodice of her dress, Celia broke free of him. She ran out from under the trees and into the sunlight. She did not stop running until she had reached the spot where they had picnicked. There she gathered up the food, hurriedly packed it away in the hamper and was waiting in the carriage for Bannock when he rejoined her.

"I think we should go now," she said, not looking at him.

"Celia—"

"Please. Let us go now."

They went, Bannock reluctantly, Celia silently. He pointed out sights of interest they passed on their way back to the Flores's ranch and she answered, when she bothered to answer at all, in monosyllables.

When they reached the ranch and she stepped down from the carriage, Bannock was encouraged by the small smile she gave him. Even the ordinary words she used to thank him for the day also encouraged him. He asked when he could see her again. Without giving her time to answer, he changed his tactics, saying, "I'll come to see you tomorrow night. Do you play cribbage?"

"What is it, cribbage?"

"It's a game. I will teach you to play it." Cribbage and other games as well, he thought as she left him and went inside. The game of love, for example, he thought as he drove away. But the words were hardly formed in his mind when he rejected them. Love was not a game. At least not love between him and Celia Flores. To him, that was a very serious matter and in no way a game.

The days that followed brought Bannock more happiness than he had known in a long time. The sound of Celia's laughter thrilled him. The way she exclaimed over small things that another woman might not have noticed, or if she had noticed them, ignored. Celia took an almost childlike delight in the things of the world, no matter how humble. He had never met a woman who was more alive. Or, to him, more beautiful, more charming, more of everything a woman should and could be.

He took her to Brownsville on a shopping trip and bought her

a hat she called "a terrible extravagance" but admitted to loving. They attended, at Celia's suggestion, a fandango held at a
Mexican homestead located only a few miles from the Flores
rancho where they danced until dawn. They parted with a passionate embrace and kisses Bannock burned into her lips, her
face and her neck before the sun could rise to spy upon them.

During those days, when Bannock was alone in Brownsville,
he continued to inquire concerning Colonel Mantavo. But he
continued to receive no or evasive answers to his queries, which
left him with a gnawing and growing sense of frustration.

Flores also turned up nothing which, at first, increased Bannock's sense of frustration. But then, as the days passed and he
continued to see much of Celia, his sense of frustration was
softened by the fact that he heard no word or even rumor of any
further depredations committed by the colonel's bravos. It was
softened as well by his growing love for the woman who had so
unexpectedly entered and made magical his life.

He was pushing her on a swing he had constructed in the rear
yard of the Flores rancho when the idea first occurred to him. As
Celia sat on the wooden plank seat he had made for the swing
and held tightly to the two ropes suspended from a sturdy
branch of a post oak tree, he continued pushing her.

Later, he let the swing glide to a halt. He took up a position in
front of Celia and said, "A few days ago when we were out at the
lake you mentioned that you used to imagine that place was
your kingdom and that you were its queen."

"Yes, I did."

"How would you like to pay a visit to another kingdom—
mine?"

"You mean—"

"My ranch. I'd like you to see it. I'd like to show it to you. You
could come up there with me and spend a few days."

He waited as Celia, staring up at him from her seat on the
swing, considered the idea. He hoped, almost desperately, that
she would accept his invitation. He wanted her to see for herself
what he had achieved over the years. He knew his pride was

involved. But there was also something more. He wanted her to see for herself what material possessions he had to offer any woman who would consent to become . . .

He forced himself to set that thought aside. He refused to put into words, even if only in his own mind, the dream that simmered inside him. To clearly state it, however silently and secretly, might tempt Fate to damage if not totally destroy the dream. He knew he was being foolish. And yet . . .

A man in love, he thought, is prone to making foolish mistakes because his judgment is, more often than not, blinded by his emotions. He didn't want to make any mistakes. Not where the burgeoning relationship between himself and Celia Flores was concerned.

"I would like very much to see your ranch," she said softly.

Her words made Bannock's heart leap. "We could go—when would it be convenient for you to come up there with me?"

"Oh, anytime, I suppose."

"How about tomorrow?"

Bannock waited. Well, what was he expecting? That she would jump at the chance to visit his ranch? That she would throw her arms around him and tell him she was ever so grateful he had invited her to his home?

"Tomorrow would be fine."

He reached out and brought her to her feet. His arms went around her and his lips met hers. Their kiss made him think of a bargain sealed.

Tomorrow!

The word resounded in his mind as he held her close and her passion intensified to match his own.

"I will see you again in a few days, Grandfather," Celia told Flores the next day at the railroad station in Brownsville as she and Bannock prepared to board the northbound train.

"I still do not like it," Flores said. "Your going away like this without a chaperone."

"I have told you many times, Grandfather. I am a modern

woman. I do not need a chaperone. Next time you will be talking
of sending me away to a cloistered order of nuns.''

"Headstrong,'' Flores said to Bannock, indicating Celia.
"Like her mother before her. You must promise me, Ben. Promise me that you will take good care of her.''

"I am only too happy to promise you that, Franco.''

The train whistle shrieked. The conductor, leaning down
from one of the passenger cars, called out, "All aboard!''

"Take good care of my horse, Franco, till we get back.''

"I will pick him up at the livery and take him home with me
when I leave town,'' Flores assured Bannock. "He will live there
like the king of horses, I promise you.''

"All aboard!"

Good-byes were quickly said and then Bannock helped Celia
climb aboard the train. Minutes later, with wheels grinding, the
train pulled out of the station, clouds of white smoke pouring
from its funnel.

"When will we get there?'' Celia asked.

Bannock told her, assuring her that the journey would not
take very long. But, as mile after mile was covered, it seemed to
him that the journey was endless, that it was taking forever. He
knew his sense of time passing altogether too slowly was the
direct result of his own impatience, which in turn was the result
of his desire to be home once again, this time with Celia by his
side.

Later that day, his desire was fulfilled. They were met at the
station in town by Viviano Colorado, who had come as a result
of the telegraph message Bannock had sent him the day before.

"Viviano,'' Bannock said, "this is Señorita Celia Flores. She
has come to visit the ranch for a few days.''

"You are welcome, señorita,'' Bannock's ranch foreman said
with a bow and a flourish of the sombrero he had doffed when
he first saw Celia. "If there is anything I can do to make your
stay more pleasant, please let me know and it shall be done.''

"Gracias.''

The ride in the carriage driven by Viviano to the ranch did not take long. During it, Bannock pointed out various sites of interest to Celia, including a herd of his cattle grazing a lush savannah and the newly installed barbed wire fencing that now surrounded his land. Once at the house itself, he helped Celia down from the carriage and, followed by Viviano, who was carrying Celia's luggage, entered the house.

"Ah!" she exclaimed once she had stepped over the threshold. "It is very nice here. Very comfortable."

"Put the lady's luggage in the south bedroom, Viviano," Bannock directed.

Later, when Viviano had gone, Bannock took Celia on a brief tour of the house's interior. When it was finished, she excused herself, pleading the need to freshen up after the journey.

Bannock left her in her bedroom and went downstairs to the kitchen where he busied himself preparing a light meal since they had both eaten sandwiches on the train. He had the food on the table when Celia reappeared.

"I thought you might be hungry," he told her. "There's some sliced turkey and some cheese. Milk. Coffee. The cook has even provided us with an apple pie."

"I think I shall have just a piece of pie and some milk," Celia said as she sat down at the table and Bannock took a seat opposite her.

"Are you tired? Would you like to turn in early tonight?"

"No, I'm not tired. I'm too excited to be tired, I suppose. *Mmmm.* This pie—it's delicious."

"One of the things that distinguishes a well-run ranch is the quality of the food provided for the men who work it. It pays, I've learned, to hire the best cook a man can get his hands on. The cook we've had has been working here for close to seven years. He's the best."

"He must like working for you since he has stayed for so long. I have heard that American cowboys—cooks too, I suppose— move about a lot. They don't, I'm told, stay in one place very long as a rule."

"Fiddle-footed."

"I beg your pardon?"

"Fiddle-footed means restless, always on the go, never satisfied to stay in one place for very long. I was that way when I was younger. Always wanting to find out what was around the next bend in the crick and over the next mountain."

"But now you are more settled, is that it?"

"There is an American expression. It says that young men have to sow their wild oats. I thought mine were all sown and harvested. I did, that is, until I first laid eyes on you. Now I'm not so sure."

Celia smiled. "Is that a threat? Must I beware of you?"

"It's not a threat. More of a promise, you might say." It was Bannock's turn to smile.

Later that night, Bannock and Celia played cribbage. The evening ended with him owing her a theoretical forty-two dollars.

In the morning, before Celia had awakened, Bannock met with Viviano to go over the affairs of the ranch and to deal with problems—some minor, one major—which had arisen during his absence.

"I have posted a man in the guard tower twenty-four hours a day," Viviano told him. "The wire, it is all in place, boss. One other thing. Sam Cavendish—you remember him?"

"He was one of the two men Wes Holbrook hired to help us protect the ranch if anything happens."

Viviano nodded. "He left two days ago. He said he hired on expecting more action and he wasn't getting it. So he drew his pay and rode out."

"Have you hired anybody to replace him?"

"No, boss, I could not find anyone willing to take his place. The men I talked to last time I was in town either do not want to hire out their guns or they do not want to fight against Colonel Mantavo and those who ride for him."

"So we're on our own."

"*Sí.* But we have much to be glad of. The guard tower"—Viviano pointed to it and received a wave from the man stationed in the tall wooden structure—"and the fence that will keep our cows safe."

"Have you heard any word of Mantavo since I've been gone?"

"No, boss. None."

"I don't know whether that's good or bad. In any event, let me say you've done a good job. Keep up the good work."

Bannock left Viviano and made his way to the cookhouse, where he asked the cook if he would prepare breakfast for two in the main house.

Half an hour later, he was sitting down with Celia to a breakfast of salt pork, creamy rice with raisins, crisp-crusted slices of brown bread, and coffee so strong Bannock remarked that he was pretty sure he could stand a spoon straight up in it.

"What will we do today, Ben?" Celia asked, looking radiant despite the early hour.

He suggested a ride out onto the range. She was amenable and so they toured the Bannock range on two saddle horses after breakfast. Its owner showed off his holdings—both the land that was as rugged as it was beautiful and the cattle that, he boasted, represented a small fortune on the hoof.

"You said to me once," he reminded Celia, "that women in your country sometimes married for reasons other than love."

"Yes, I did. It is the way in my country."

"Celia, I don't know how to put this so I reckon the best thing for me to do is just to plunge right in and get it out. I'm not a poor man as you can see. I am a man who needs a woman in his life. For a long time I didn't think that was so. But since I've met you—now I *know* it is so."

"Ben—"

"Wait. Let me finish. I'm asking you to marry me, Celia. I'm also promising to give you a good life if you'll do that. You'll not want for anything, that's a promise. One I'll keep. You can count on it. I—"

"Ben, we have only just met."

"What difference does that make?"

"We do not yet know one another very well."

"I know you, Celia. And I've tried to be open and aboveboard with you so that you would get to know and understand me. How long does a person have to know another person before he decides he wants to spend the rest of his life with that other person as I do with you?"

"Ben, you have taken me by surprise. I cannot give you an immediate answer to your proposal. I need time to think."

"Celia, I'm in love with you. Are you—I've got to ask you this. Do you have any—feeling for me?"

"*Sí.* I do. You are a fine man, Ben Bannock. You are kind and considerate. You are brave. You would make some woman a fine husband."

"Some woman," Bannock repeated glumly. "But not you?"

"I didn't say that."

"But you won't agree to marry me."

"Not now. Not this minute. As I have told you, I need time to think. Time to consider your proposal."

"How much time?"

Celia smiled and reached out to gently touch Bannock's cheek. "You are an impatient—even an importunate—man, Ben."

He sighed. "I reckon I'll just have to do what I have to do. Which is wait for you to make up your mind."

"Thank you, Ben."

During the remainder of the drive, Bannock forced himself to speak with false heartiness of his land, his stock and his plans for the future—which included expanding his holdings and importing blooded Durhams from the east to crossbreed with his long-horns to improve the overall quality of his stock.

Celia was as hearty in her responses to his plans. She encouraged him and assured him that he was bound to succeed in the future as he had in the past.

But Bannock's mind was only partly on their conversation. The other part, the major part, was on Celia's response to his proposal of marriage. He tried while talking of other things to think of ways to make her change her mind. To accept him and all he had to give her. He was sure that she was as attracted to him as he was to her. Their embraces, their kisses, were warm, even fiery at times. He came at last to the only conclusion he could reach which would, he reasoned, explain her hesitancy.

Colonel Pedro Mantavo.

It was Mantavo, Bannock was now convinced, who stood between him and Celia and the realization of his goal—marriage to the most desirable woman in the world. He wanted to ask her if what he was thinking was correct but he did not dare to so much as mention Mantavo's name. He feared talking of the man because to do so, he suspected, might serve to drive Celia closer to Mantavo and farther away from him.

That night after supper and another game of cribbage, Celia rose, yawned and then apologized for her weariness.

"The air today—it was so fresh and invigorating. It has quite worn me out, it seems."

Bannock got to his feet and walked her to the foot of the stairs leading to the second floor. When she hesitated there, he gently took her in his arms and kissed her almost chastely.

Her reaction was not chaste but passionate. When their lips parted, she looked up at him and, seeing the somewhat surprised expression on his face, said, "I never said I didn't love you, Ben. I never said I did not desire you."

"Celia, I want you so much—" He kissed her again.

Suddenly, she broke free of his embrace. He was about to ask her what was wrong when she took his hand and led him up the stairs and into her bedroom.

In the morning, alone in the kitchen while Celia still slept, Bannock marveled over the events of the preceding night. He had been surprised to find that she had never before been with a man. He could still hear, as he stood gazing out of the kitchen window while cradling a hot cup of coffee in his hands, the sharp cry of pain Celia had given when he . . .

But that cry of pain had quickly given way to murmurings of love. She tenderly whispered, over and over again, a lilting litany of love as she held him and he wished she would never let him go.

Surely now, he thought, she will agree to marry me. But later, when Celia came shyly into the room, her eyes averted from him, he found it impossible to speak to her of marriage. She looked as if she might bolt were he to do so. She seemed almost frightened of him.

"Celia, about last night—"

She put a finger to her lips to silence him.

But he ignored the gesture. "I hope you're not sorry about what happened between us."

"I am confused," she murmured.

"Confused?"

"My feelings—I do not know what to do with them. I do not know what they truly are. Sometimes I feel one thing, sometimes quite the opposite. I am not experienced where men are concerned other than to flirt and to tease. But now—you and I—"

He waited expectantly for her to go on but she said no more. Not until they were finished with breakfast. Then, "I think it would be best if I were to return home today, Ben."

"But, Celia—"

"I need some time to think, as I've told you. You can come to visit me—"

"When?"

"In a few days."

"You're sure you want to see me again?"

An expression of surprise tinged with dismay appeared on Celia's face. "How could you doubt that? Especially after last night?"

Relief flooded Bannock at her words. He reached out and took her hand.

"I'll go upstairs now and pack my things."

Bannock restlessly paced the floor as he waited for Celia to return. He was still pacing when a loud knock sounded on the front door. He went to it and opened it.

"Señor Bannock?" inquired the young male Mexican who stood outside with his hat in his hands and a horse behind him.

"Yes, I'm Ben Bannock. Who are you?"

"Manuel Bolivar, Señor Bannock. My father sends me here to give to you the message."

Bannock, puzzled, stared at the young man whose name he had not recognized.

"You do not know me, señor?"

Bannock shook his head. "Should I?"

"My father, he is a friend of Don Franco Flores. Don Flores comes to my father and says he must send me to you with the message."

"Of course!" Bannock exclaimed, suddenly recognizing the name the young man had given him. "Your father's Paco Bolivar. Don Flores has mentioned you both to me. You say you have a message for me?"

"What is it, Ben?" Celia asked as she reappeared beside him. Then, recognizing Manuel, she greeted him and asked him what was wrong.

"Your grandfather, señorita, he say to my father that he must send me here to tell Señor Bannock that Colonel Mantavo, Don Flores has heard, is sending some men here and when they come they will kill Señor Bannock and destroy his rancho."

"When are the men coming?" Bannock asked.

"That Don Flores says he does not know but he thinks it will be soon. He say I am to tell Señorita Flores she must leave this place at once and return to her grandfather's house with me on the train. I came north on the train and then I rent a horse to ride here to warn you, Señor Bannock."

"Manuel," Bannock said, "I'll give you a carriage you can drive into town and leave at the livery there. Take Señorita Flores with you. You can travel by train together back to Brownsville."

"That I will do," Manuel said firmly.

Bannock yelled for his ranch foreman, who came running out of the bunkhouse and up to him.

"Viviano, get a carriage ready for this young man and Señorita Flores. They're driving into town." As Viviano headed for the barn, Bannock turned back to Manuel. "I thank you for coming here to warn me. Tell Don Flores and your father I thank them as well for sending you to me."

"I will go and help get the carriage ready," Manuel volunteered. Leading his horse, he went sprinting toward the barn Viviano had entered moments earlier.

"Ben, come to Brownsville with me," Celia said. "If what Manuel says is true—"

"He'd have no reason to lie to me."

"Then you must leave here or you might be killed. In Brownsville—or at my grandfather's house—you would be safe."

Bannock shook his head. "I can't leave here now. I have to stay and defend my home and my property." He hesitated, giving Celia a speculative glance. "I thought you didn't believe any of the stories that have been going around about your friend, Pedro Mantavo."

He saw the fire flash in Celia's eyes and immediately regretted having made his remark.

"I do not believe rumors. They are often only old wives' tales with no truth in them."

Unable to stop himself from perversely pursuing the matter, Bannock added, "You heard what Manuel said. Mantavo's ordered his men, according to rumors your grandfather has heard, to attack my ranch. How is it that your grandfather believes the rumors he hears about Mantavo and you do not?"

Celia closed her eyes. Her teeth began to worry her lower lip. Then, opening her eyes, she said, "I refuse to fight with you. I will ask you just one more time. Will you come south with Manuel and me so that you will be safe?"

"Celia, I can't."

"You mean you won't."

"Yes, I reckon that is what I mean. But if I did go, would you have any respect for me then? For a man who cuts and runs with his tail between his legs at the first sign of trouble? I don't think so."

Instead of answering Bannock's question, Celia picked up her luggage and left the house as Viviano drove a carriage up to the front door, Manuel Bolivar seated beside him, Manuel's rented horse tied behind it.

Viviano stepped down and let Manuel take the driver's seat. He helped Celia into the carriage and then handed up her luggage.

Celia looked at Bannock, who was standing in the doorway watching her. "Ben?"

He hesitated. He silently swore. Why did the world turn in such a way that forced a man to choose between the woman he loved and the estate he had sweated and slaved so many years to create?

Again, "Ben?"

Gritting his teeth, he shook his head. "If all goes well, I'll come to visit you in a few days as we arranged—if that's still all right with you."

Celia sighed. Nodded. "Take care of yourself, Ben."

"Vaya con Dios."

Manuel waved to Bannock and then drove away.

Bannock, watching them go, felt a blend of rage and longing surging within him. Rage at Colonel Pedro Mantavo for what he was planning to do and longing for the woman he felt he was losing by the immensely difficult choice he had just made. Losing? Or had he already lost her? Still another troubling thought occurred to him. Had Celia Flores ever been his to lose in the first place?

Bannock set his unhappy thoughts aside and turned to Viviano, who was watching him with a curious expression on his face. "That young man who was just here—he brought word from a friend of mine down near Brownsville that Mantavo is sending some men up here to raise Cain. I want you to ride out and talk to all our hands. Tell them we're expecting a raid. Any man who doesn't want to risk his neck, I'll pay him off and he

can ride. Those who want to stay and fight—get them back here
along with the stock in a hurry. We've got to get ready for
whatever it is that's coming."

"It will take me some time to get the word to all our boys,
boss. A few of them, they are up on Bear Mountain summer-
pasturing the stock. Chuck and Denny are fixing fence over east
of Little Gulch and there's a bunch that are haying down near
Parson's Bend."

"Round them all up as quick as you can, Viviano."

Without another word, the ranch foreman headed for the
corral behind the house. Minutes later, he was riding out aboard
his buckskin.

Bannock strode over to the base of the guard tower and
knocked on one of its wooden supports with the butt of his
revolver. When the guard, a man named Dusty, in his perch
high above the ground leaned out to see what the matter was,
Bannock called up to him, telling him about Manuel Bolivar's
message and cautioning him to be on the alert for sign of any
riders approaching the ranch.

"Which way do you reckon they'll be coming from, boss?"
Dusty shouted down to Bannock.

"Can't say for certain. But my guess is they'll be coming from
the south."

"I've got a bell hung up here, boss. If you hear me ring it, you
all come a'running."

Bannock went inside the house and unlocked his gun rack.
Nine rifles, most of them Winchesters. He took boxes of ammu-
nition from a drawer and proceeded to load each of the weapons. Then he left the house and went into the barn. In the loft,
he found bales of hay stacked nearly to the roof. He opened the
door of the loft and then proceeded to haul bales of hay and
throw them down to the ground. He was sweating when he had
finished his self-appointed task and sweating even more heavily
by the time he had hauled the bales of hay into position to form
a waist-high barrier between the snake pole fence and the
house.

That's two barriers they'll have to breach, he thought as he surveyed his handiwork. The fence'll slow them down and so will that breastwork I've built.

He went back to the house to wait for the men to return but he found he was too restless to remain where he was. He went back outside and climbed up into the guard tower where Dusty was scanning the surrounding countryside, a .44-caliber Winchester in his hands.

"No sign of a soul anywheres around, boss," Dusty declared, looking not at Bannock but at the horizon to the south. "Maybe it'll turn out to be a false alarm."

"Maybe. But I'm not counting on it."

"Right you are not to. Like folk say, 'Better to be safe than sorry.' "

The two men were silent then, each of them watching for any sign of approaching strangers. Dusty finally broke the silence with, "Here comes a bunch." He pointed.

Bannock stared at the band of horsemen galloping toward the ranch. "They're our men," he said as they came closer and he could make out faces.

He climbed down from the guard tower and was waiting for them when the men rode in.

"Heard there's going to be hell to pay around here, boss," a man named Cass said. "Viviano told us about it out where we were haying near Parson's Bend."

"When the cattle get here," Bannock said, "bunch them up over there in the west. Set two men to riding herd for two hours on and two hours off."

"The greasers are after the stock, are they, boss?"

"The stock—and me."

Cass muttered an oath. "They'll have to get past us to do you in, boss, so there's nothing for you to fret about. Until the cows get here, we'll man this here hay-bale breastwork in case anybody shows up before the cattle do."

Cass and the other men rode around the house to the corral. When they returned, they were on foot. They took up positions several yards apart behind the long line of hay bales Bannock had placed between the fence and the house.

"I'll watch the back," he told the men and left them. Once behind the house, he began to march back and forth, one hand resting on the butt of his gun. His pacing reminded him of another time and another enemy in another war. How many times as a younger man during the War between the States had he done guard duty on the perimeter of some desolate military camp with only the stars and maybe an owl or two to keep him company? The more things change, he thought, the more they remain the same.

It was close to eight o'clock that night when the sounds of bawling cattle could be heard in the distance. Bannock left his post and rounded the house to find his stock heading toward the house at a fairly fast pace. He climbed up on a bale of hay and yelled instructions to the men driving the herd.

They promptly obeyed, turning the herd to the left and driving them west to what would be their bed ground for the long night ahead.

When the cattle were in place and the first shift of night herders posted, Bannock returned to the rear of the house to resume his pacing.

He heard not a sound in the night. No nightbird called. No owl hooted. The cattle were quiet. He almost relaxed.

When the bell in the guard tower began to clang more than an hour later, he was having trouble keeping his eyes open. The alarming sound sent him springing into action. When he saw no one behind the house, he sprinted around to the front. As he did so, the guard in the tower yelled, "They're coming! From the south!"

At first, Bannock could see no one in that direction. But he could hear the sound of horses' hooves pounding the ground. Then, in the light of the flames flaring from the barrels of guns being fired by the advancing marauders, he caught brief glimpses of mounted Mexicans heading his way.

His men returned their fire as did he. Soon a pitched battle was taking place. The bandits dismounted and took cover. One who had tried to jump the snake fence while still in the saddle lay dead between the fence and the breastwork of hay bales. His horse wandered west, occasionally spoiling the aim of one or more of the ranch's defenders.

"There's a whole host of them out there, boss!" Cass yelled and squeezed off a round. "There's more of them than there is of us, that's for sure and certain." Cass sent another round keening into the darkness.

Bannock crouched down behind a bale of hay and propped his gun on top of it. Squinting into the night as he tried to pick out a target, he was totally unprepared for the assault that was suddenly launched upon him and his men from the rear.

Mexicans came racing out through the front door of the ranch, their guns aimed at the startled men they had taken by surprise. Other Mexicans smashed windows on either side of the door and thrust their weapons through the openings they had made.

"Drop your guns!"

Bannock recognized Diego Anza's voice. He rose and slowly turned to face the man.

TEN

"DROP YOUR GUNS!" Anza repeated.

Bannock's men glanced at him and then back at Anza. Slowly, they dropped their guns.

"You too!" Anza barked, taking aim at Bannock.

Bannock reluctantly tossed his gun onto the ground.

Anza grinned. Then he yelled into the darkness. "Come on in!"

Minutes later, a horde of Mexicans came bounding out of the darkness to climb over the snake fence and then the hay-bale breastwork.

As Anza ordered, "Get their guns," there was a scramble among his men to gather the guns and pile them in front of their leader's feet.

"You should have protected your rear, Bannock," Anza said. "You put all your guns out front and that was a bad mistake. When we arrived and saw that you were armed and ready to fight, I took some of my men, circled around your left flank and came up behind your rancho."

Bannock wanted to lunge at the man, get his hands around Anza's throat and throttle the bandit leader until there was no life left in him. But even in the heat of his rage he realized that part of his fury was really directed at himself for having made a serious tactical mistake: his failure to protect his rear. But he had been sure that the men attacking from the south constituted all of the invading force. As Anza had said: a mistake. A serious miscalculation.

"Bannock, you should not meddle in other men's affairs," Anza told him in a schoolmasterish tone. "We would have had many fine horses for Colonel Mantavo to sell if you had not come upon us and driven us off the other day. When I told the colonel what had happened—it was then that he decided you must die."

Bannock's eyes dropped to his gun lying in the pile with the other weapons his men had been forced to surrender.

Anza noted the glance. "You would not try anything foolish would you, Bannock?"

"If I get the chance, Anza, I'll kill you. With my bare hands, if necessary."

Mockingly: "If you get the chance . . ."

"I'll stop you, Anza. You and Mantavo—all of you. Next time I get word that you're planning something—"

"Next time you get word? What is it you mean by that, Bannock? Does it have something to do with the fact that you were ready for us when we came here tonight?"

Bannock said nothing, wishing with mute desperation that he could take back the words he had just uttered.

Anza walked up to him. He placed the barrel of his revolver under Bannock's chin and tilted the gun upward, forcing Bannock's head up so that their eyes met. "Speak to me. Tell me what made you get ready for us tonight? Did someone inform on us? Did someone learn of our plans and tell you of them?"

When Bannock remained silent, Anza swore and struck him on the left cheek with the barrel of his gun, drawing blood.

"You are a stubborn man, Bannock. Stubborn men are troublesome. They are like steers that will go their own way, no matter what, and cause trouble for all concerned."

Anza's stern features softened in a slow smile. "I have said that I came here to kill you. That is a true thing. But before I do what I came here to do—some sport might be in order."

Anza beckoned and one of his men hurried to his side. He spoke in a low voice to the man who went scurrying toward the adobe tack house that stood next to the barn.

"Build a fire," Anza ordered two of his men, who went to the three-sided shed where cords of wood were neatly stacked. They brought back enough to start a fire which was blazing by the time the first man returned from the tack house with a branding iron in his hands.

Anza gestured and the man placed the end of the iron that bore the Double B brand in the fire.

Bannock watched it grow slowly red as the flames heated it. He was still watching it when Anza gave an order in fast Spanish and two men seized him from behind. They dragged him over to the boardwalk fronting the house. There they tied him to one of the stout timbers supporting the overhang. One of them reached out and ripped open Bannock's shirt to bare his chest.

Anza removed the iron from the fire and held it up in front of him as he advanced upon Bannock. "This is hot enough, do you not think so, Bannock? You are a cattleman. You know that an iron heated beyond a dull red will burn too deep into the flesh of a cow—or a man. Campfire red. That is the color that will produce an even brand, one that would in time, were I to let you live long enough—which I will not do—produce a brand the color of a new saddle's leather because it burns off just the outer layer of skin."

Bannock struggled to free himself. He strained at his bonds as Anza moved the brand closer to his bared chest. He wanted to tear his hands free, seize the glowing iron in Anza's hand and use it to brain the man, to beat him senseless and then crush his skull.

But the ropes that bound his hands behind his back held and he could not so much as move his back away from the wooden support to which he was tied.

Anza's swarthy face, the scar that marred his forehead, the drooping black mustache he wore, the man's wide-nostriled nose—every feature of the outlaw's face was imprinted indelibly on Bannock's mind as the leader of the renegades moved closer to him—so close he could feel the heat of the dull red iron on his skin.

His head involuntarily slammed back against the pillar as Anza rammed the brand against his bare chest. He gritted his teeth to stifle the scream that was rising in his throat in response to the agonizing pain the glowing iron caused him as it burned away his skin.

Then, as Anza, grinning and chuckling softly to himself, held the iron firmly in place, Bannock could not help himself. As pain spread outward from his savaged chest to, it seemed, every nerve in his body, his mouth flew open and the scream he had been fighting to suppress burst from between his lips.

The awful sound continued, anguish and agony blended in it, even after Anza took the iron away from Bannock's burned and smoking chest, which now bore his own Double B brand.

Anza's laughter blended with Bannock's scream in an ugly, if brief, symphony of sound. Then he dropped the iron on which shreds of Bannock's charred skin still sizzled and turned to his men.

"There was, I saw, whiskey in the house. Brandy. Bourbon. Wine. Some of you—guard those guns." He indicated the guns he had forced Bannock's men to give up. You two—guard those men. If they move a muscle, drill them. The rest of you—it is time to celebrate our victory over this Bannock I have just barbecued."

His men's laughter seemed to please Anza as he strode with them into the house.

Bannock, his teeth grinding noisily together, dropped his head until his chin touched his chest just above the burned portion of his flesh. Slowly, he slid down along the pillar until he was sitting on the edge of the boardwalk, his legs sprawled out in front of him.

He closed his eyes, squeezing them shut, as he tried to will the pain away—and failed to do so. It blossomed in his chest like some obscene flower which, in its growing, seemed to send fire

shooting into his brain as well as his chest. He was barely conscious of the sounds coming from inside his house. The sound
of shattering glass. The sound of many men singing in Spanish.
He sat there on the edge of the boardwalk, his arms aching and
his wrists chafing due to the tightness of the rope that bound
them.

A wave of dizziness washed over him. He felt as if he were
falling while at the same time realizing that could not possibly
be, bound to the pillar as he was. And yet, the feeling persisted.
To try to banish it, he opened his eyes. At first, the world around
him seemed to sway. Then it steadied and he saw his men
gathered together in the distance under guard. They were
watching him. Was it pity he saw in their eyes? Horror?

His gorge rose bitter within him, bringing nausea in its wake.
He swallowed hard and then swallowed again.

He did not know for sure how much time had passed when he
heard a faint scraping sound coming from—where? At first, he
couldn't pinpoint it. But then, as the sound persisted, he knew
where it was coming from. It was coming from the narrow space
beneath the boardwalk on which he sat.

A whisper: "Boss?"

"Viviano!"

"I came back from Little Gulch with Chuck and Denny. We
see what is happening here. We circle around behind the house
where no one is."

Despite the pain that was still racketing through him, Bannock could not help but smile. So he was not the only one who
made serious tactical mistakes. Diego Anza did too. He had also
failed to protect his rear, sending men to guard only the Bannock ranch hands and the pile of guns lying on the ground some
distance away and not the northern perimeter of the house.

"Are Denny and Chuck under there with you?" he asked in a
low voice in order not to be overheard by the Mexican guards
who were talking and laughing together and, as far as he could
tell, paying no attention at all to him.

"We leave our horses out of sight in back behind the barn.

Denny and Chuck and me, we sneak up to the locust trees on the north side of the house. They stay behind the trees while I crawl along the ground and then under the boardwalk. Boss, can you turn around?"

"Turn around?"

"So your hands, they will face south. You do that, I can cut the rope that binds them with my knife."

"I'll do it," Bannock said resolutely. "I'll *do* it!"

He immediately began to try to shift his position. It was difficult to do, he quickly discovered, because the two men who had tied him to the pillar helping to support the overhang had left little slack in the rope. But he kept trying. He strained at the rope, pulling himself forward, his arms stretching painfully. He managed to ease an inch to the right and then a little farther in that direction.

"Boss?"

"Give me time, Viviano. It's a tough task, believe me. My arms feel like they're going to rip right out of their shoulder sockets."

He continued trying to turn his body so that his hands would be accessible to Viviano. Slivers sliced into the flesh of his arms as he did so. Sweat beaded on his forehead and ran down into his eyes, causing him to try to blink the salty water away.

"Can you feel my hands?" he muttered several minutes later.

"*Sí,*" Viviano whispered as his fingers touched the flesh of Bannock's hands and then proceeded to use his knife to slice through the rope that bound them.

When, minutes later, the rope fell away, Bannock had all he could do to keep from leaping to his feet and shouting his joy into the night sky. He eased his body around until he was sitting in the same position he had been in before Viviano's arrival.

"We make a plan, boss, Denny, Chuck and me. I was to come to free you. Then you would call the guards. Say something like you are choking. Anything to make one or more of them come to you. Then I will come out from under here and we will kill them. Chuck and Denny will come running and the other men will grab their guns and it will all be over soon, *sí.*"

Maybe yes, Bannock thought. Maybe no. The best laid schemes of mice and men . . . He saw the muzzle of a revolver protrude from beneath the boardwalk, a shadow among shadows. Surreptitiously, hardly moving at all except for his right hand, which snaked toward the weapon, he took the gun and held it hidden behind his back.

"Hey!" he yelled. And, *"Hey!"* again.

The three guards turned toward him, frowns on their faces.

"What do you want, señor?" one of them asked silkily. "To go to the outhouse, perhaps?"

Laughter.

"Water," Bannock called out to them. "I want a drink of water."

"He wants a drink of water," one of the two men guarding the ranch hands said to his companion. "Carlos," he called out to one of the men standing guard over the guns. "There is a well. Give the señor a drink of water. Go, Carlos!"

Carlos hesitated and then went over to the well. He lowered the wooden bucket into the well and then cranked it back up again. Resting the bucket on the stone rim of the well, he took the dipper down from its nail and filled it with water from the bucket. Carrying the dipper, he headed for Bannock, who was watching him closely.

"You want water, señor?" Carlos inquired as he stopped in front of Bannock, who looked up into his hard eyes and nodded. "Then it is water you shall have."

The last word was no sooner out of Carlos's mouth than he threw the water the dipper contained into Bannock's face.

Bannock sprang to his feet, seized Carlos, spun him around and placed the barrel of the gun Viviano had given him against the side of his captive's head.

"Don't draw!" he yelled to the other startled guards whose hands were going for their guns. "You do, you're dead!"

Out of the corner of his eye he saw Chuck and Denny abandoning the cover of the locust trees and running, guns in their hands and cocked, toward the front of the house.

"Get your guns," he yelled to his men as Viviano emerged from under the boardwalk. The command was unnecessary because his ranch hands were already sprinting toward the spot where their guns were piled on the ground.

"Diego!" one of the guards standing frozen in the distance cried. *"Diego, help!"*

At the same instant, Carlos tried to break free of Bannock. The attempt failed when Bannock clubbed him on top of the head with the barrel of his gun and the Mexican crumpled to the ground where he lay without moving. Bannock turned sharply as Anza and the others with him came storming out of the house, some of them with bottles clutched in their hands.

Anza went for his gun.

Bannock squeezed off a round that winged the man. Apparently unfazed, Anza fired at Bannock but missed because Bannock had dropped to one knee as Chuck, Denny and Viviano began firing at the Mexicans clustered around their leader beneath the house's overhang.

A Mexican screamed as his hands flew out and back and the bottle he had been holding smashed against the stone wall of the house. As the man went down, Anza dropped to the boardwalk and propped the lifeless body of his bravo up to protect himself from the shots that were still being fired at him and the men with him.

As the gun battle raged on, gunsmoke turned the air acrid and the fire bursting from the barrels of revolvers lit the night like ragged red stars.

The men clustered around Anza bolted. They ran into the house, their leader right behind them, and slammed the front door shut. Seconds after their flight, they began firing at Bannock and his men from the broken windows of the house.

Viviano, who had taken cover behind a bale of hay returned the fire and then ran to where the Mexican guards were being held under the gun by one of Bannock's men. He said something to the man that was not audible above the continuing firing and then he and the man each seized one of the Mexicans and, using them as human shields, began shoving them roughly forward toward the house.

Viviano's ploy failed. The Mexicans firing from inside the house promptly shot their two companions. As the two dead bodies sagged to the ground, Viviano and the man with him dived for the cover of the hay bales. Viviano made it but the man with him did not. He went down with a grunt as a round slammed into his chest.

Viviano crawled toward Bannock's position and, when he reached it, said, "This will go on all night, boss, unless we can storm the house. They've got stone walls between them and us."

"A rear guard action," Bannock muttered.

"What—"

"You go to the left. Take Chuck and Denny with you. I'll go to the right. We'll meet behind the house. Stay down. Don't let Anza or anybody else see what you're doing or where you're headed."

Viviano ducked as a bullet whined over his head. A grin illuminated his face. "We do like they do when they come, eh, boss? Come in at the back door."

"Well, my friend, it's like the old saying goes. 'What's sauce for the goose is sauce for the gander,'" Bannock quoted.

"Let us hope the good God lets us roast those geese inside the house."

Bannock and Viviano parted, heading in different directions.

When Bannock reached the end of the line of hay bales, he hesitated for a moment and then darted out into the open. He ran in a northerly direction, his legs pumping and his breath coming in short shallow gasps. In the distance, he could see Viviano and two other men running in the same direction.

Once at the rear of the house, he halted and quickly surveyed the scene. No bravos in sight. Good. He eased along the back wall of the house, his gun in his hand and aimed straight ahead. He had not gone far when Viviano, accompanied by Chuck and

Denny, rounded the other end of the house and began moving toward him, their guns also in their hands.

When they all reached the door, they stood there for a moment listening to the sound of gunfire coming from the front of the house and then, at a signal from Bannock, they burst into the house and raced through the kitchen and on into the living room.

They spread out as they entered the living room and Bannock yelled, "Stop firing!" To prove he meant business, he put a round into the wall next to Anza, who was crouched next to the open door as he fired at the men outside.

Anza's response was a feral snarl and a squeezed-off shot that almost downed Bannock.

Viviano, Chuck and Denny sent a volley of shots into the room, several of which struck three of the bravos, killing two of them and wounding one.

But Anza, undeterred by the surprise attack, leaped to his feet. With his legs spread for balance and his gun gripped in both hands he sprayed the room with lead, killing Chuck instantly but missing Bannock, who took cover behind a high-backed mohair chair. Viviano, who threw himself to the floor, and Denny, who had taken shelter behind a door, were unhurt.

"Don't shoot!" one of the Mexicans cried, dropping his gun and raising his hands.

"We surrender!" another bravo cried, imitating his companion's actions.

"Your gun, Anza," Bannock said, holding out his free hand as he leveled his own weapon at the man whose eyes were wild and whose cheeks were displaying a hectic flush.

"Damn you, Bannock!" Anza shouted, and was about to squeeze off another round.

He never got the chance.

Bannock put a bullet in the man's brain.

As blood spurted from the large exit hole the bullet had made in the back of Anza's head, splattering the wall behind him, one of the Mexicans, his eyes wide with fright, crossed himself and murmured a garbled prayer. But the others turned and, firing aimlessly in their alarm, ran out the front door—and into a burst of gunfire from outside.

Bannock stared down at Diego Anza and felt a sense of grim satisfaction flood him. He looked from the corpse near the door to the still powerfully painful Double B brand burned into his chest. He would, for the rest of his life, have something to remember the man by. With his jaw set and his eyes ice, he stepped over Anza's body and cautiously peered outside where the gunfire had stopped. He called to his men, who rose up from behind the bales of hay where they had taken cover and hailed him.

"Looks like it's over, boss," one of them called out. "Sorry to say, some of those greasers got away from us and are probably already across the border, they were running that fast."

"It's over," Bannock confirmed, gazing at the bodies littering the ground outside. "Now it's time to bury the dead and be done with it."

Three days later, after repairing the damage done during the attack on the ranch and working out a detailed plan of defense with his men in case more bravos returned, Bannock fidgeted impatiently in his seat aboard a southbound train.

Did absence truly make the heart grow fonder, he wondered as he thought about Celia Flores whom he was on his way to visit. Or was it true what people said: "Out of sight, out of mind"? He forced himself to sit still and stare out the window. But the scenery drifting by outside did not register on his consciousness. Instead he saw an alluring image of Celia Flores. Smiling at him. Beckoning to him. He fiercely willed the train to travel faster.

When at last, after what had seemed a week-long journey to him, Bannock stepped off the train in Brownsville, he hurried to the livery stable where he rented a two-seated carriage. On the drive out to the Flores ranch, he imagined Celia sitting beside him as they talked of their plans for the future. They would do many and marvelous things together. They would have healthy, happy children. Their days would be filled with a happiness Bannock was sure would be greater than any he had ever known before, surpassing even that which he had shared with Nora. He heard himself confessing to Celia that, since meeting her, he had come to realize that his life had been, if not exactly empty, at least lonely. He told her he wasn't sure now why he had gone on. He didn't know what had made him get up in the morning day after ordinary day and do whatever needed doing. Now— now that he had met—and fallen deeply in love with—her, his life had taken on a meaning that turned everything he saw or touched into something marvelous. Even the most ordinary things—a sunrise, a hot cup of coffee, the sound of someone's happy laughter—all these and everything else that shared the world with them had, for Bannock, been turned into the stuff of dreams and delight.

He used the whip the farrier had given him and his horse went galloping along, the noise of its hooves hitting the ground almost but not quite drowning out the sound of Bannock's whistling.

It was Franco Flores who opened the door later that day to Bannock's knock. The old man's face remained impassive at the sight of his unexpected guest.

"How are you, Franco?" Bannock inquired, offering his hand.

"Your horse is well," Flores declared without shaking Bannock's outstretched hand. "He is in the barn."

What's wrong, Bannock silently asked himself. Why won't he look me in the eye? "May I come in, Franco?" he asked aloud.

Flores gave him no answer. But he did step aside and allow Bannock to enter the house.

"Is Celia at home?"

"She is. She has a guest."

Flores led Bannock into the living room where he found Colonel Pedro Mantavo seated on a sofa next to Celia, his large hands enclosing her delicate ones.

Mantavo looked up as the two men entered the room. So did Celia—and then she immediately lowered her gaze.

"I'll come back," Bannock said, "some other time."

He started to leave the room when Celia said, in what he thought was a strained voice, "Don't go, Ben. I have something to tell you."

He stood there, his back turned to her, and then, with a sense of dread burgeoning within him, he turned to face her.

She opened her mouth to speak and then closed it. She glanced covertly at Mantavo.

Bannock's gaze shifted to the colonel. Mantavo was dressed as if for a special occasion. Gold braid adorned his velvet *chaqueta*. The front and cuffs of his embroidered shirt were embellished with the finest of Cholula lace. His *pantalones*, bell-bottomed and gusseted with yellow silk, were tight across his strong, lean thighs, after the manner of the *charro*. The leather holster which held his pearl-butted gun was exquisitely tooled, carved and stamped. On his ring finger flashed a large ruby.

"Señorita Flores," he said softly, "seems at a loss to tell you, Señor Bannock, what it is she wants you to know. I am sure that is because she is overwhelmed with her suddenly changed circumstances. Excitement and anticipated pleasure have quite overwhelmed her."

"Celia, what is it you want to say to me?" Bannock asked.

"Pedro—" she began. "Colonel Mantavo has asked me once again to marry him and—and this time I have consented to do so."

Bannock stood as if turned to stone. He could not take his eyes from Celia's face as she stared at him. His world came crashing down around him without anyone else in the room seeming to notice the disaster taking place.

He glanced at Flores, who avoided his eyes.

"Your men might as well have killed me earlier this week as they damn well tried to do," he said huskily, addressing Mantavo. "You've done as much by taking from me the woman I love."

"The woman you love? Celia loves me, Señor Bannock. Has she not consented to marry me?" Mantavo turned to Celia and squeezed her hands in his. "Tell him, my darling."

Celia hesitated a moment and then, "It is true, Ben."

"What is true?" Bannock exploded, his hands fisting at his sides.

"I love Pedro," Celia said. "I am going to marry him."

"It is perhaps for the best, Ben," Flores suggested in only the ghost of his usually strong voice. "One should marry someone of one's own kind."

It was—Flores's words were—the final blow for Bannock. "Celia," he cried, hating the sound of pleading that colored his tone, *"I'm* your kind!"

She sat there, rigid, silent.

"You—you're going to marry a man that would order his men to destroy my ranch as he had destroyed so many others, a man who employs men who would do a thing like this?" Bannock ripped open his shirt to reveal the still-raw wounds of the Double B brand he now bore in the center of his chest.

Celia gasped. Her face paled.

"Diego Anza did this to me!" he continued, his eyes fixed on Celia's face. "And Diego Anza rode for your intended before I shot him—for *him.* " His hand shot out, his index finger pointing at Mantavo.

Did Celia whimper? He wasn't sure.

"I am weary of unfounded accusations," Mantavo interjected. "Especially those made against a man who is no longer among the living and thus unable to defend himself."

"So you know Anza's dead," Bannock said.

"I know that he is dead, *sí.* I also know that some of the other men who rode north with him a few days ago are also dead. Killed by—"

"Me and my men killed them," Bannock interrupted when Mantavo's words faded away. "And you damn well know it, Colonel. You no doubt heard it from the lips of those bravos of yours who got away from us."

"I know nothing of that," Mantavo insisted. "But this I do know. I know that men like yourself, Señor Bannock, would do well to mind their own business as I have told you before. Men who meddle in the affairs of others—sooner or later, their meddling must come to a stop—or be stopped."

"Is that a threat, Colonel?"

Mantavo shrugged. "If you are having trouble in the north, Señor Bannock, why are you here and not there attending to it? That could prove to be a very bad—maybe even a fatal—mistake."

"Damn you, Mantavo—"

Flores quickly stepped in front of Bannock and forcibly prevented him from attacking the colonel. "Please, Ben, you dishonor me when you dishonor a guest of mine."

Bannock fought to control his anger, his fingers flexing at his sides. "I'm sorry, Franco," he muttered. "Not about wanting to kill that man but because I almost did it here in your house." He stepped back and said, "Celia, I want to talk to you."

She looked at Mantavo. For approval? Then she rose and left the room.

Bannock followed her outside. He came up behind her and put his hands on her shoulders. She did not immediately move away from him. He thought, in fact, that she leaned back toward him, an almost imperceptible movement, but he could not be sure, upset as he was. Then she moved forward a few paces and turned to face him.

"There is nothing to say, Ben."

"I think there is. I think there's a whole lot to say. To start with, I want to say I love you. You know I do. I want to marry you. We—"

"Ben, please. Do not put me through this torment. I have made up my mind. I will be married in a few weeks. It was good knowing you. I will always remember it as a very pleasant interlude in my life."

Bannock stared at Celia in disbelief. "Is that all it was? A very pleasant interlude in your life?"

"We can be friends, Ben."

"No!" He turned away from her. "No, we *cannot* be friends! If you marry that man—how in the world do you think we could ever be friends? I could not stand to be in the same room with the two of you, knowing that you belonged to him, that he—" His head dropped. "No," he repeated. "No, no, *no!*" He turned on his heels and stared at Celia. "You know that man has tried to have me killed by the likes of Diego Anza and the men who rode with him. He has caused the deaths of some of my men. How, Celia? Tell me how we can be friends if you turn from me to him? If you know, tell me, because I do not know."

Celia sobbed, her hand rising to press against her lips. "Go away, Ben."

"Celia, it's not too late. It's not too late for you to change your mind. We can still go away together. We wouldn't have to stay in Texas. We could go far away. To a place where Pedro Mantavo would never find us. Celia, I can't live without you. I don't *want* to live without you. Please. Won't you change your mind? Won't you give me a chance to prove to you how much I love you and how good our lives could be together?"

Celia shook her head almost violently. "No," she managed to murmur as tears filled her eyes. "Go away, Ben. Go away and never come back here!"

"All right. Now that I think I understand—all right! I'll go. It's clear to me now what you're doing. You told me so yourself.

"You said that people in Mexico—your people—often marry for reasons other than love. They marry to obtain power, you said. Or money. That's it, isn't it? You're marrying Mantavo because he is a powerful man in Mexico, a rich man as a result of his rustling and other illegal enterprises. You don't want me. I'm not powerful. And it seems I'm not rich enough to suit you either."

"Stop it!" Celia cried, the shrill sound of her voice a step short of a scream. She clapped her hands over her ears and lowered her head. "I will hear no more of this. *No more!*"

He stood there helplessly, his heart breaking, and watched
her run from him.

When she had disappeared inside the house and slammed the
door shut behind her, he made up his mind to go after her and
apologize for the things he had just said to her. Then he would
—somehow he would find a way to make her understand how
very much he loved and needed her. He would find a way to
make her change her mind . . .

His shoulders slumped. It wouldn't work. He knew, to his
sorrow, that it wouldn't. Love could not be forced. If she didn't
feel for him what he felt for her, then there was no point to
pursuing and arguing with her. To follow that course would be
worse than futile. It would turn what was now clearly her sorrow
and regret over the way things had worked out between them to
anger and bitterness that would only serve to alienate her from
him to a still greater degree.

He went to the barn, looped a length of rope around his bay's
neck, gathered up his gear and returned to his rented carriage.
He tied his horse to the back of the rig, tossed his saddle and
other gear into the carriage and then drove away from the
Flores ranch without once looking back.

On the evening of the day following his visit to the Flores
ranch, Bannock rode north, trying hard to think of nothing. Not
of the raid on his ranch and certainly not of Celia Flores. But his
efforts failed. Both subjects dominated his thoughts and both
distressed him.

He finally succeeded in forcing them out of his mind as he
continued his northward journey under the star-studded sky
above him. He turned up his collar because of the cool wind that
had begun to blow. An hour later, it was that wind that made
him aware that something was wrong. It carried the too-sweet
stench of rotting flesh.

He stiffened and stood up in his stirrups, surveying the shad-
owy countryside surrounding him. A few minutes later, he saw
the first of the many dead cattle scattered about his home range.

He rode up to them, thinking of streams and springs poisoned with arsenic by Mantavo's bravos. But when he reached the first of the bloated corpses, he saw bullets had lodged in the bodies. He rode the range, finding more and more dead cattle, all of them shot to death. A chill coursed through him. He spurred his bay and went galloping north.

Another ominous signal borne by the wind reached him. He recognized this one too. The throat- and nose-searing stench of smoke.

His heart sank when he came within sight of what little remained of his ranch. Only smoke-stained stone walls and the stone chimney.

All the rest was a mass of charred timbers, piles of black ash and twisted metal. He drew rein and dismounted. He stood there for a moment staring at the total devastation.

"Hands up!"

The familiar voice startled him. "Viviano?"

"It is you, boss?"

"It's me."

Bannock turned to find Viviano approaching from behind the ruins of the barn that still smoldered. He lowered his hands.

"Bravos," Viviano said in a lifeless voice. "They came back, boss. This morning. Before dawn. There must have been fifty of them. Maybe more. We didn't have a chance. They killed most of us, boss. Some of the men got away as did I. They have not come back. I came back to wait for you to return."

Bannock drew a deep breath. "He's won."

"You mean Colonel Mantavo?" When Bannock nodded, Viviano continued, "One of the bravos, he shouts that you must serve as a lesson for any other rancher who would dare to fight against *el Colonel.*"

Bannock was having trouble absorbing not only the extent of his losses but the very reality of them. Celia Flores. His ranch. His cattle. Everything of value was gone.

"You will begin again?" Viviano asked tentatively. "You will rebuild?"

Bannock shook his head. "No. This time it's finished."

"What will you do? Where will you go?"

Bannock had no answer for either question. He shook hands
with Viviano, swung into the saddle and rode off into the darkness.

Bannock picked up a stick and used it to stir the campfire. His
action sent sparks flying up into the darkness.

He looked up at the boy, Tony, who was watching him intently. "Sorry I drifted off like that. I was taking a turn down
memory lane and remembering a wonderful woman I once
knew. She was my kind of woman. A beauty with brains. She was
so beautiful she could have lured a man into a burning building.
Too bad things didn't work out between Celia Flores and me.
Too bad she had to up and marry an arch-enemy of mine."

"You're wrong about that."

"About what?"

"Celia Flores didn't marry Colonel Mantavo. Or anybody else
either, for that matter. The colonel was killed while raiding a
Texas horse ranch before the wedding could take place."

Bannock stared at Tony in a state bordering on shock, unable
to voice the many questions that were suddenly whirling about
in his mind.

"She did not mourn Mantavo," Tony continued, "because he
had tried to have you killed and because she did not love him. It
was you she loved and she had told that to Mantavo. She told
him you had asked her to marry you and she had decided to do
so."

"Then why did she change her mind and decide to marry
Mantavo?"

"He forced her to agree to marry him. He found out that her
grandfather, Franco Flores, was informing on him and his plans
to you. He swore he would kill her grandfather unless she
agreed to marry him. He also swore he would kill anyone to
whom she might turn for help against him. To protect her
grandfather, she agreed to marry him."

"How come you know so much about the affairs of the Flores family?"

"Because I'm a part of it. My mother, Celia Flores, told me she tried to find you after Mantavo was killed but nobody knew where you'd gone after his men had burned down your ranch and slaughtered your stock.

"She christened me Antonio. Once I was old enough, she told me all about you and her. Over and over again. She liked to say that I was born bearing the Bannock brand. When I grew up, I decided to come hunting you. In town today I heard about the fight you were in there. Nobody knew your name but a man told me your shirt had gotten torn in the fight and he saw the Double B brand that my mother told me Diego Anza had burned on your chest. So I right away set out to trail you . . . and here I am."

Bannock, unable to find the words he wanted to say, decided that it was just as well because he didn't trust himself to speak to his son, whose eyes, as blue as his own, were staring fixedly at him.

"I thought," Tony continued, "maybe now that I've finally tracked you down we could head back to the border. I know my mother would be more than happy to see you again after all these years. She's always told me that the Bannock brand wasn't burned only on your chest but also on her heart—had been ever since the day she first met you."

"You're real sure about that, are you?"

"I'm sure."

Bannock looked away for a moment, his heart bursting with a sudden and almost overwhelming happiness, and then back at Tony. "The border's a far piece from where we are at the moment. I'd say we'd best start for it come first light."

They did, riding side by side, heading for a reunion with the woman Bannock intended—at long last—to marry.

About the Author

Leo P. Kelley is the author of the popular Luke Sutton series of Double D Westerns. Some of his other Double D books include *Morgan* and *A Man Named Dundee*. He lives in Long Beach, New York.